White Clyffe

By

Colin Fletcher

colin@foxhangers.co.uk

Grosvenor House
Publishing Limited

The right of Colin Fletcher to be identified as the author of this
work has been asserted in accordance with Section 78
of the Copyright, Designs and Patents Act 1988

The book cover is copyright to Colin Fletcher

This book is published by
Grosvenor House Publishing Ltd
Link House
140 The Broadway, Tolworth, Surrey, KT6 7HT.
www.grosvenorhousepublishing.co.uk

This book is a work of fiction. Any resemblance to
people or events, past or present, is purely coincidental.

A CIP record for this book
is available from the British Library

ISBN 978-1-83975-557-6

CONTENTS

PREFACE by Colin Fletcher.

After many years of writing local history notes, both as a discipline and for memory support, I thought I might tell the story as fiction. I was, however, quite sure the characters must be the story, while the history remained the background against which they lived.

The fourteenth century was incredibly turbulent, for a people quite unable to manage a deteriorating climate and an epidemic that raced across the known world. A savage loss of population led to a shortage of men and boys to control the plough, and a shortage of families to bake the bread.

The landowners were in disarray but could not manage the new situation. They were astonished by the Peasant's Revolt which spread as a raging fire from Kent and Essex to Bridgewater in the west and to Yorkshire in the north.

The Characters.

John and Joan spend their life on a small farm at White Clyffe a few miles north of Calne below the Marlborough Downs. Their first children, Edith and Edwin were born during the Great Famine; their growth stunted by malnutrition. Wilfrid and Juliana an unmarried brother and sister lived together in middle life, while Morris the youngest son had three sons and two daughters. Hilda, a sixth child was a sickly girl who died late in the second year of the Black Death when John and Joan began to hope they had escaped lightly. Their eldest son Edwin rebelled against his stubborn inflexible father and left the farm to work in the cloth trade in Salisbury, but all of the others continued to live nearby.

The Steward, a military man when younger had fought in the Welsh Wars during the later years of the previous century. Now he was pushing his aging body around the countryside managing nine agricultural estates for his Lord.

The Widow Alice, attracted to the Steward, managed the Big House after a long period of neglect. Now the house was warm, clean and well stocked with provisions when the Steward arrived with his team of young men.

The Village Reeve, with no friends in White Clyffe was a solitary figure. His position between the Steward and the unwilling villagers who increasingly resented the rigid control of their lives, left him completely isolated.

A Wandering Priest, an illegitimate son of a landed family was an engaging man and an entertaining speaker who could hold any audience till he became bored. He travelled widely through Wiltshire and the neighbouring counties as a wandering beggar monk but with enough nerve to pose as a legitimate priestly figure in country towns; he belonged anywhere but nowhere.

Charles the Clothier also born of a good family but with insufficient land, had developed a substantial weaving business near Bridgewater. Salisbury was the most important marketing centre for the trade, and he determined to establish a business there also. Travelling widely throughout the West Country he was aware of a smouldering resentment and feared the consequences for villagers.

The Spymaster lived a life in the shadows in Salisbury, feeding the military with information, which he obtained from weak and vulnerable people susceptible to bullying and a promise of cash.

PROLOGUE by Edith, a market trader.

My dear father brought us up hard; he had no choice. I remember nothing before my fourth birthday, but I do remember we were always hungry, for these were the famine years... everyone was hungry, and we children were all small and skinny. Seven bad years, Dad told me, and everyone else said the same.

A bit later I remember the Steward, a fierce old warrior, from the Welsh Wars he told me. "King Edward wanted a full-time army of foot soldiers, but no one yet understands how this will change our villages," the Steward said.

Well, now we have the Peasant's Revolt. Is that what he meant? And now my own poor nephew, missing, perhaps gone from us all, no one seems to know what happened.

CHAPTER ONE

A Priest and a Village Boy.

John was a wiry lad, about twelve years old, already worn by hard labour.

His young brother lay in the little churchyard since March when the pale, delicate primroses came into flower. John had picked some a few days later and spread them on the bare earth but they soon wilted. Now, later in the season when the flowers had gone over, he had dug some plants up by the roots and was now planting them on the grave.

A small man dressed in a shapeless black garment watched him silently, then turned away to the side gate. He should have stopped the boy, and would have when younger and more energetic, but he needed to get away to his own crops down by the river. The wheat never thrived down there in a wet winter and he had re-sown the bare patches with spring barley, but now weeds were threatening the new seeds. The Priest was a good farmer and had double ploughed the lower strips to bring the ridges higher and hoped to improve his crops; it was a great satisfaction to him to see a good crop.

John stood up. The numbness had left his young mind now, replaced by acceptance, and he remembered the blond curly head of his little brother fondly; that curly head of hair loved by matrons everywhere. But he too must get off to work, the cow is bellowing and the hungry calf calling for its first feed of the day. As he walked back towards home, a mist was rising from the river and the sun on his back warmed him gently.

John milks the cow and lets the calf join her for a few hours. His father emerges from a small, thatched house collecting the square wooden bucket of milk, most of which will be used to make cheese.

He walks with difficulty for he is a tired man even at first light. His wife, John's mother, is long gone and Jane only comes in to tidy the house twice a week; she has her own young children to care for.

The house is one of a dozen standing beside a rough track, only now recovering from winter traffic. Behind the house a small paddock, a hayrick, a few trees, and a vegetable patch provide some insurance against starvation and give a sense of comfort to father and son. The cow is tethered near the trees and is nibbling the new growth of weeds and grass; the hungry calf is sucking hopefully and will continue to do so throughout the day.

Some days the cow must join the plough team for several hours and the anguished calf must bear the separation. West field had been planted mostly with wheat at the end of last year, but it had been a wet winter; the later planting had germinated poorly and very little had survived in waterlogged soil between the ridges. After the crops of barley and oats had been planted in April in freshly ploughed soil, according to the agreed plan, the Reeve brought them together to see if the failed wheat crops could be re-planted. Grain was scarce at the end of a long winter and few people could spare anything; only two of the larger farmers who might have taken their surplus to market, were able to provide seed corn.

The poor smallholder whose crop had failed had already lost two bushels of seed, but rather than grow nothing had reluctantly agreed to share the crop with the man who provided the seed; half the crop was better than nothing. The Priest has watched the proceedings as an apparently neutral referee. Later he is seen talking to both farmer and smallholder suggesting a portion of the seed be donated for the love of Christ. The cautious men demurred but offered something, "If the oats come to harvest".

The Priest was always there at every event within the village and knew all the families; he baptised them and buried them. Some villagers were friendly, others reserved, John's father simply broken; but the boy might be saved.

"John, I want you to do something for me when you have finished your work. Come to my house tonight." The boy was not keen but dared not refuse.

As evening light faded John left the little farm and walked to the Priest's house. It was quite dark when he knocked on the door and he stood anxiously, for what felt like an age, till the door began to creak and slowly move on bad hinges.

"John, you have the knock of a rent collector, but come in."

A wax taper beside a short row of books gave the dimmest of light, but slowly he saw a low wooden stool beside a bench. The Priest sat himself down while John stood uneasily.

After a long pause the Priest said, "Did anyone see you come?"

"No–o, weren't nobody about."

"What I have to say is important but must be a sacred trust between ourselves. Do you agree? Lay your hand on the Bible now."

John did as he was told and repeated the priest's instructions, scarcely understanding why.

"John, I will teach you to read the Bible."

John was stunned. He knew no one, old or young who could read the Bible, except the Priest. Why should he need to know how to read? It was not natural, and perhaps dangerous. He absorbed the need for secrecy in that moment.

"On Sunday you will help me with the service and after everyone has gone, we will have our first lesson."

On the next Sunday when everyone had left the church after the service, the Priest took John to a quiet corner at the back of the tiny building. He read a familiar passage from the service in Latin that John recognised and was encouraged to repeat.

John stumbled and mumbled his reply. The priest repeated the short phrase and John tried again. Gradually after several attempts there was some improvement. The Priest took a piece of chalk and wrote the first few words on a slate.

"Now John, look at the slate and tell me what the first word sounds like."

"No–o, I cain't do tha–at."

The Priest repeated the phrase and said, "Now you repeat what I have said and look at the slate while you say it."

John was confused by the words on the slate, which meant nothing at all to him. He could no longer remember the words that he had recited earlier and became more and more upset. Eventually the priest saw he had to calm the boy; together they prayed for divine help. John walked out of the church into sunshine and birdsong with a profound sense of relief.

Sunday after dreaded Sunday the process was repeated; but there was no improvement. After several weeks, the Priest was ready to abandon the experiment.

"Well, John, we aren't doing very well, are we? What will you do when you leave here today?"

"Oh, I'll see if the cow is alright."

What is the cow like?"

"The cow is brown."

"Where will she be on a hot day like this?"

"Under the tree."

"What colour is the tree?"

"The tree is green."

"So, the cow is brown, and the tree is green?"

In a moment, the Priest wrote on his slate and passed the two rows of words to John, saying, "The cow is brown. The tree is green."

John recited the same to the Priest with a weak smile. He looked at the words as he spoke, and the Priest pointed at the words as he did so; after a few weeks John became completely familiar with these six words and sometimes would scratch them in loose soil with a stick. Always he took the greatest care to scuff them out before anyone saw them.

Summer came and summer went, and the days grew shorter. The Priest was most uneasy on the first of January 1313 and again on the thirteenth of January 1313; he had prayed longer and more fervently than usual. A low sun sent long shadows across crisp white snow; he shivered and fingered his beads while children played noisily, quite oblivious to his concern. The harvests that year and the next were difficult but survivable, and for most people hunger was not fatal, but the climate had been deteriorating throughout the new century and crop growing was less successful now. There were just too many people living in this village, and in every other village.

When work allowed, John walked with friends to neighbouring villages and the little town nearby. On one of these journeys, he notices a quiet girl, less foolish than her boisterous companions, but is too shy to talk to her.

A few weeks later he sees her again; recognition encourages him to smile; they chat briefly. During the long days of summer there was little time to go a-walking but after harvest they met again when the motherless girl could leave the young ones. As the short days passed the evenings grew longer and hopes began to rise with the season. In March John picked two primroses and gave them to the grave and thoughtful girl. He answered the unspoken question, "One for you, one for me. Keep them close together."

CHAPTER TWO

Famine.

Throughout 1315, from April till August it rained almost every day, weeds flourished among the wheat, barley and oats and soil stuck tenaciously to the villager's feet. This awful year was followed by another, then by two more slightly less foul, followed by further failed harvests. One person in six died prematurely in the worst famine in English recorded history.

After the longest day, small areas of grass were cut for hay in any short spell of fine weather. On the next dry day when the weathered grass had dried a little, it was shaken by hand and the green grass in the bottom of the swathe was exposed to the elements. This was repeated between rainstorms till the discoloured and half made hay was stacked into a row of small weather-proof heaps across the field, resembling those small groups of sheaves seen in the wheat field since the dawn of remembered time; they called them pooks. John would recall this dispiriting summer and the next till his last days. One Sunday evening while everyone was at church the cow had escaped from her tether and intoxicated by freedom, had attacked the neat row of heaps flinging them high in the air with her long curving horns.

For a few days early in September the rains ceased and everyone in the village came to the lord's wheat fields controlled by the Reeve, a villager like themselves. He had managed the village workforce for twenty years, like his father before him and his authority was only rarely challenged, but he was no one's friend.

Later in the day the more fortunate villagers could work on their own land, but the landless cottagers worked till nightfall under the control of the reeve on the lord's land or the reeve's own land. They would need to be paid with grain to have any hope of surviving the winter, and some would not live to see the spring. They showed their children how to rub the grain from the ear when no one was looking, then chew it into a life-saving paste.

John wondered how the grave and thoughtful girl was managing and sometimes visited her in the next village. He was usually able to take a rabbit or a young pigeon from the nest, and this was accepted silently; they were prepared together for the pot on the fire which produced a daily supply of thin soup.

He lingered for as long as he dared in the soft company of the attractive sisters. The girls grew thin, and thinner still after Christmas. In March, their father took the last of the grain to sow the spring crops. After two weeks slender green shoots emerged in the cold damp soil inspiring hope of better times, but long hungry months stretched ahead.

John brought small amounts of grain and hoped his father would not notice, once he trapped a wild duck and later in the season, they picked wildflowers to season the tasteless pottage. In June, as they walked together, he slipped his arm around her waist and to his amazement, she responded hungrily. In August he spoke to her father and quite quickly they married. In March, Joan gave birth to a daughter who they christened Edith.

They were living with John's father now who enjoyed having Joan in the house with her energy and good humour. She took on the milking of the cow and they often made the cheese together except for a few weeks after the baby was born. When a second baby was born a year later, conditions became cramped in the little house and she began to think of building a second house at the end of the garden plot.

The house was very small, and no one quite knew how old it was. There were still some houses in the village that were built of timbers dug into the soil and these had to be rebuilt after twenty years or so when the main timbers rotted at ground level and the roof sagged.

But the wall timbers of their little house were built into a raised bank which extended the life of the building. Stone was scarce in this district, but a few large stones had been found to sit under the main posts. They had been dragged for a considerable distance on a simple wooden sled behind the cow a generation ago, perhaps by John's grandfather. Unavoidably, the earth bank had sloped into the living area and reduced the floor space.

John and Joan discussed this problem with other villagers, and someone suggested a low cob wall that surrounded the garden of a great lord's house about ten miles away. After haymaking in July, they left their two young children with one of Joan's sisters then continued to the distant village. There they found the garden wall and asked one of the villagers how the work had been done. "Oh, t'were a few year ago, now. I dunno who dun it, mind."

At length they found an old man who had worked on the wall, "T'were jist mud zno. We packed it in tight an' let un dry. Corse it had to be thatched to keep the rain off un".

Fired with excitement the young couple started back on the long walk to collect their children and return home. "Well, we got mud awright and we can mix it with cow dung and straw an' maybe a bit of cow hair will help bind it in I spec."

But soon they were into the harvest with an even greater sense of urgency after two years of severe hunger. The mornings were taken by the lord on the manor farm as ever, under the management of the Reeve, but later the villagers with strips of land in the common fields could tend their own. John's uncle came to help with the less arduous work, but John, seventeen years old, had strength and stamina for two and would continue cutting corn till after dark. The next afternoon, Joan brought Edith and Edwin to the cornfield. While she joined John and his uncle, Edith looked after her baby brother, sometimes struggling through long stubble to find her mother when he cried too long. Joan swept her up in her arms with a broad smile and together they returned to find the baby. The entire family worked long into the evening enjoying the sun and the smell of dry, brittle corn. As the sun went down Joan found the children fast asleep in the straw and returned to the house, while the men lingered chatting to other villagers working nearby.

Throughout the day they had made the mown corn into sheaves, then hiled them up into a single row of little stacks along the crown of the ridge, each containing eight sheaves. After two or three days standing in sun and wind, they could be brought to the paddock behind the house to start making a corn rick, followed by a second acre a few days later.

Following two years of near incessant rain they were torn between making a protective covering of thatch for the rick of new golden corn or pressing on with cutting the next strip of standing corn. Usually, the thatching had to wait for a day too wet for harvesting. This intense programme of hard labour would continue throughout August and frequently into September, but there was no greater happiness than the sight of stacks of good grain, securely covered against the worst weather that winter could bring.

Here and there, a widow or an injured man would be helped by friends and neighbours, all desperately anxious for themselves and their families, but the best of them would help the more unfortunate, led and encouraged by the Priest.

Two slightly better years were followed by three more years of utter misery, aggravated by a worsening shortage of seed, so crops were thin even before they were damaged by heavy rain and cold sunless days. Wheat was particularly vulnerable though oats and rye were slightly more adaptable, however grim bread from any source was welcomed. Even a family with acres in the common field like John and Joan, were affected. A third baby lived only a few weeks. Joan was so thin and frail she had no milk. The baby sucked hungrily on a piece of woollen rag soaked in cow's milk but grew weaker by the day.

The Priest sought to comfort her, "My dear children, life is natural, death is natural." For weeks she hardly had the strength or the will to care for the older children. The three-year-old daughter became protective of her little brother and even tried to help John when he came in from work, exhausted and depressed.

Violent crime was widespread and not restricted to stealing food. Breeding livestock were often eaten in desperation and the slow expansion of villager's herds and flocks was reversed. During the desperate years, the safety of the tiny herd was a constant worry, and a lean-to shelter was built against the house to keep the animals secure at night and this also provided shelter and warmth, reducing losses from disease. John and Joan were afraid to leave the farm; desperate men grew hard and bitter.

The Sunday services were a particular anxiety for John, who was still assisting the Priest. The children were frequently sent out of the church to check if all was well, and if any strangers were seen, men poured out of the door, followed by the priest who shared their concern. The strangers, had they known, would have been terrified to learn that the men would be expecting to be called for pike drill after the service and had left their pikes outside the church, leaning against a yew tree in the churchyard.

CHAPTER THREE

The Steward.

The Steward was a military man, or had been when young and vigorous.

He had fought in the Welsh Wars during the later years of the previous century, a long, arduous and magnificent campaign when soldiering became a permanent occupation. The part-time conscripts who always wanted to return home to harvest the crops, just when the enemy was at its weakest and most vulnerable, had been unable to dislodge the Welsh fanatics from their treasured land. The mounted knights had the means to fight for most of the year, but a significant force of foot soldiers was needed in that filthy terrain.

The Steward was a very junior member of the landowning class; the third son of a father who was himself the youngest of many. There was simply not enough income from their modest land holdings, so the family had been drawn to the military world for generations. The development of a full-time army had been great boost to people in his situation.

Now he ached painfully after hours in the saddle, and his master would have him visit all of nine estates four times each year and he knew that in three months between visits many things could go wrong; he was always hurrying to another place further along the road. When he did reach the estate, much depended on the memory of the Reeve, who might be assisted by the Priest as cleric, for who else could keep a written record in the village.

He arrived at the big empty house with a small group of riders who led the horses to the rather dilapidated stables, only to discover that no hay had been provided, nor had a fire been lit in the harness room. After a long hard day tempers were frayed, and only after a good deal of shouting, did men appear around the ricks in the yard behind the stable, to cut trusses of hay for the horses.

"This should already have been ready in the loft, you damn fools, God knows you have little enough to do."

"Nobody told I you were cummin."

"Well just get on with it, double quick. And we want these saddles and bridles dried out, so someone get the fire going. And the thatch is bad on this roof, so bring some thatching straw tomorrow."

In the big house the Steward was kicking the table leg discontentedly. An old servant shuffled in with a few sticks.

"Good God, man, have you nothing drier than that? Who looks after this house?"

"Bain't bin no one ere fer months."

Which the Steward knew well, for a lived-in house was a rare luxury. How he missed a woman's touch on his travels, and not just for a warm fire and a good meal. Smoke rose from a tight bundle of straw and a little flame tickled some small twigs of ash. Dry bark and larger sticks were added and within ten minutes a respectable fire in the open hearth brought some cheer to a November afternoon.

"Who is helping you with the food? And we will need some new bread, and plenty of it," though they always carried fresh bread, having been caught in this situation before. "That fire should have been in all day."

"Well nobody told I you were cummin."

"Just get on and bring the women. We'll have nothing for hours as it is. And bring the Reeve as well."

"E bain't ere. E be gone to Calne, all day."

A few hours later, the house has warmed up and a hot meal of ham and beef and bread has cheered everyone. The women raised everyone's spirits and had eaten well themselves, and now they were being offered as much good beer as they could drink. The steward had caught the eye of a slightly older woman and they chatted comfortably.

"I be a poor widder woman wi no one to look atter I."

He was sympathetic, "I'll look out for you if you are good to me."

"Well, I got to get through a long winter wi not much work about."

He toyed idly with a silver coin; her hand slid towards his. "When I leave, you can have it."

"In the mornin?" Alice sought confirmation.

"No, we are here for a week."

"Well one in the mornin then, an one at the end of the wik."

He smiled for the first time and she looked into his eyes, warily at first then responded, lightly patting the back of his hand.

"Nuther beer, m'lord?"

"Oh aye, and another for you."

Much later they staggered to a pile of straw covered by a layer of sheepskin and fell into a drunken sleep still wearing their heavy outdoor clothes. Sometime later one disturbed the other, who responded happily and tenderly. Before daybreak they woke again and her arm was around the back of his neck, their wet lips and tongues searching each other hungrily and strenuously without a care who heard them. After twenty minutes he was completely spent and snoring noisily. She eased herself away from him, drew her clothes around herself and went to the fire to bring it back to life.

She started to work the dough, pausing to place some hot ashes from the log fire into the bread oven. Later, when the younger men came in from feeding the horses the smell of new bread put an edge on their appetite.

"Ah, you jist wait. Baint ready yet mind."

"Well, don't keep 'em waiting, we have a long day ahead." But there was no malice in the Stewards voice. The old servant appeared with logs for the fire.

"I want to see the Reeve, first thing. Where is he?"

"I han't sid im."

"Well you better find him and bring him here."

An hour later, the Reeve came to the big house, and Alice met him outside.

"How be ee?" the Reeve asked.

"Better now eve slep well," she said with a cheeky grin. The Reeve was too anxious to smile back, but slightly relieved, all the same.

"Oh, ah."

"They be yer for the wik mind."

The Reeve paused before speaking, "Ah, they'll do both places from ere then. But you look atter him an maybe I'll find summat for ee when they be gone."

Inside the house the Reeve found the Steward with a mouth full of bread and was himself overcome with a spasm of coughing. The food was hurriedly cleared from the table.

"God, I hope you are not going to die on me. We've got a busy week."

The Reeve nodded and grunted something unintelligible.

The Steward again, "How much wheat have you threshed?"

The Reeve reflected then spread the fingers of one hand, and again and after a slight pause a third time. Then a longer pause, "Eighteen quarters, I reckon."

The Steward, briskly, "I want to get some to Salisbury, there's a good price, they are short of wheat. How many carts and teams do you have?"

A longer pause for calculation, and further coughing. "I shall have to look at the carts but might be three I reckon."

The Steward, "Well that'll be six quarters then, but I want to get ten there." Turning to the young men, he said, "Ride over to Stoke and see if they can make two loads, we can take five carts together and you can ride to Salisbury with them. Well move then, while you've got a bit of sun."

Out in the yard, the Steward and the Reeve walked past the barn where two men were threshing wheat on the wooden floor. The long flails lifted above their heads were brought down swiftly against a sheaf of wheat. They worked to the same rhythm, one man raising his flail as the other came down to the floor, but at an easy pace that could be sustained all day.

A thatched lean-to shed contained the oxcarts. These were inspected for leaks in the floor which could lose grain all the way to Salisbury.

"Better take some wet clay with you to stop any new leaks. It will go bad for you if you don't get all the wheat there."

The Reeve nodded for it seemed to be a friendly warning. The threshed grain was stored in a guarded room in the main barn, and both men now looked at the sample. Later the Reeve supervised the measuring and bagging. The grain was shovelled into a square bucket which held exactly one bushel; two bushels were tipped into each bag with great care. The carts were each loaded with eight bags, making two quarters in total.

The Reeve then chose the men he wanted for the journey, including John, who was excited by the prospect of the journey to Salisbury, a fabled city, growing like a mushroom in the meadows around the cathedral.

Later that day he spoke to Joan, "What? What? Wha-at? You can't possibly leave me with the children and now we've got three cows to milk. How can you go?"

John was not completely surprised by her reaction and suggested she get someone to help with her work while he was away. He also pointed out that he would not have to do as much day work at the manor during the weeks after their return. He could then start to extend the house that would give them the extra space they needed to store the increasing quantities of cheese they were making.

Next morning before daybreak, teams of four oxen were hitched to each cart and two more oxen were tied behind one of the carts in case of lameness or injury to the teams. The sacks of corn were carefully placed to balance the two-wheeled carts, then covered with waterproof skins. The carts also contained food, water, tools and heavy staves for each man to deter thieves, together with an old bugle from the Welsh Wars.

As first light the convoy moved off with one of the Steward's men on horseback plus the Reeve riding an old heavy horse that had probably not got into a gallop for years. The Steward's man was armed and three miles down the road they met the other group from Stoke with a second armed guard; memories of the famine years were still fresh.

They reached Calne in less than two hours, the market town now becoming busy. Most people stared at the unusual convoy and wondered where it was bound, and why were they not selling their wheat in Calne at the Friday market, like anyone else. A mile out of town they stopped at the foot of the long steep hill rising to the Marlborough Downs.

The pair of idle oxen were brought to the first cart and hitched up to make a team of six, and they set off one cart at a time. But this was too slow, and they sent a team of four up, allowing them to rest part way up, and the others followed suit, sometimes assisted by men pushing the carts to help the oxen. On level ground on top of the downs, they rested for half an hour having the first main meal of the day, enjoying the unusual view of Calne far below.

Off again and it was an easy walk on level downland, known to them all since boyhood adventures years ago. Soon the Pewsey Vale came into sight before and below with a clear view of Etchilhampton Tump in thin sunlight. This descent was much less steep than the climb from Calne, but the men needed to be ready to push their staves through the spokes in the large wooden wheels as a primitive brake. There was a risk that the loaded cart might push the oxen forward, a stumble and a fall could easily lead to a broken leg. They all knew this, but it did not stop the Reeve shouting a warning several times as they proceeded down the slope into Bishops Cannings.

They made camp before dark below Redhorn Hill so the oxen would be fresh for the climb up to Salisbury Plain. This would be the last watering point for the oxen before Shrewton unless they could find a dewpond holding water near the track. They unhitched the oxen, tethered them for grazing and lit a fire between two rows of carts. Their bread was growing stale now, but tolerable with plenty of beer. The Steward's young men and the Reeve sat a little apart from the villagers whose conversation was loud and lubricated as the hours passed. Eventually the Reeve took control of the beer barrel, joking that we would need to save some for the next night. Two men stood guard for two hours, minding the cattle and watching out for potential thieves, till relieved by a second pair.

A third pair counted the oxen in the dark, checked all the carts and at the first hint of light to the east, kicked the fire into life, roused the sleepers and prepared a rough breakfast. The oxen had fed well overnight and were taken to water by men chewing dry bread themselves. This would be the last chance of water today. The first team to be watered was sent up the hill, the last major climb on this journey. One by one the carts were brought up on to Salisbury Plain and the convoy eventually went off in close order.

This was new country to most of the men though the Reeve had made the journey before with his father. Not a house in sight, nor another traveller passed by. Once a flock of sheep was seen being moved away from the track by a reclusive shepherd. It was a grey morning and a raw wind with only a few thorns to break the monotony of the endless grassland. But it was a gentle undulating route and the oxen meandered comfortably at a stately two miles an hour. Late in the afternoon they came down from the hills into Shrewton where water and freshly baked bread would be found.

The remainder of the journey into Salisbury was made along river valleys closely settled and farmed; John now understood that the hills seemed so desolate because all the villages were hidden away in narrow valleys, a strikingly different landscape from the wooded clay country north of Calne. After an overnight rest at Shrewton, the oxen were permitted to stop and feed along the side of the track so they might arrive at Salisbury with a full belly.

The city was busy and noisy and quite smelly for open drains ran down the middle of the streets. New houses and workshops were being built and loads of stone, timber and straw competed for the inadequate roads without order or control. Iron shod cartwheels bounced and clattered on flint and broken stone. The shattering noise from the weaving shops had an almost physical impact, doors and windows were open to the street to try to ease the torment within. Everything was conducted at the top of the voice in the vicinity of these workshops and the cloth trade was the single largest business throughout the city.

The Reeve seemed to know where he was going and led the convoy by shouting and waving, till they reached the corn market. The carts were unloaded quickly into secure storage and there was just time to return to the outskirts of the city where there was water and grazing for the cattle. No one was to be paid till they returned to White Clyffe, so the young men had no possibility of succumbing to temptation in the city.

But almost 400 feet above this mayhem, the glorious spire of the cathedral stood serenely, new stonework gleaming, demonstrating the superiority and grandeur of the church. For all the novelty that John had encountered on this journey nothing compared remotely with Salisbury Cathedral whose majesty seemed to reassure his religious belief. His childhood acceptance had been tested during the appalling years of the famine, during years of widespread suffering that were far beyond the ability of anyone to relieve.

The Steward's men had galloped off as soon as the grain had been placed into store and the number of bushels had been recorded. The Reeve returned to the city in the morning to oversee the auction and the convoy made their own way back to north Wiltshire.

Chapter Four

Family Progress.

Edith and Edwin survived the long famine, but their growth was restricted by malnutrition. A child born in 1324, lived to adulthood; three more in the next ten years also lived, but of the six children only two produced children of their own. Edith was always concerned for her energetic and adventurous brother and feared his scrapes and falls; he loved to run away and hide, listening to her frantic calling. Though a year younger, Edwin was soon able to outrun her, and Edith was frequently seen in pursuit in the village street, the distance between them slowly increasing. The good mother in her compelled her to watch him playing endless games with a bundle of sheep's wool, which a group of village boys would pursue and kick for no apparent purpose; at least in this group neither of them was at a disadvantage, for the entire generation was stunted.

John had persevered with his reading of English and started his own children at an earlier age; in the course of time all of them could write their own name, sometimes they would write messages in the dirt to each other. The usual name form was Edwin son of John and curiously Edith son of John, this often spoken as John's son. As surnames became necessary in later years the family name became Johnson.

During the next two decades after the famine, John and Joan raised their large family with an iron will and great care. The succession of disastrous harvests did not occur again, but their life was never less than a daunting struggle demanding a tough and resilient mentality. Slowly, almost imperceptibly, they prospered.

The years of sustained rainfall enabled weeds and grass to grow abundantly and more cattle could be raised. The minority of villagers who owned a cow, such as John and Joan, were able to rear a calf most years. The birth of a calf is a thrill for the whole family that owes nothing to financial security or base ambition or fear of starvation; it is a new life, an elementary joy. Even the most ancient, gnarled, grizzled farmer will stroke the calf as tenderly as a new mother, and John was no exception. He returned to check the cow and her calf four or five times in a few hours; later in the evening he came out of the house saying he would, "Just have a last look before bed."

Next morning, he rose early and would do nothing else till he had checked the calf again. Then, and only then, did he stoke the fire, boil some water and dunk the burnt crusts from yesterday's bake to make his hot morning drink.

Joan joined him beside the fire and asked, "How is the calf?"

"Fine, fine, nice little heifer, sucking well."

As weeks became months the calf grew stronger and when out in the paddock by day, she was tied to a log of wood. Soon she had eaten all the grass in a circle around the log and was compelled to stretch for more grass when she discovered she could drag the log. Not only did she reach new grass, but she could also reach her mother's udder; no longer could the cow lie peacefully in the shade feigning deafness while the calf bleated pitifully for her mother's milk.

All calves, male or female were trained to pull the log from their earliest days preparing for a life in harness to the sled, a wheeled cart or as a member of a team of eight drawing the great plough. The village teams often used cows for ploughing alongside steers to make up the numbers so the cow was far more useful than a steer to most villagers because it also produced milk and most years a calf; but it demanded more feed to do this.

Yet reality intervenes, and survival compels a commercial approach. Heifer calves could be reared and would produce calves of their own. Additional milk would be made into cheese and after a few months of maturing, be sold in the market at Calne. The male calves could be trained for the plough and be sold for a substantial sum, perhaps to replace an aging steer in the plough team on the demesne farms of the lord, or the gradually increasing herds of the most fortunate villagers. As ever, the landless cottagers remained vulnerable with few opportunities to improve their position, limited by their ability to work and to develop their skills.

A reduced population survived in the village after the famine, but little land became available and the market price of wheat remained high; the supply of grain was still barely adequate to feed the reduced population. John continued to assist the Priest and after his father's death became better known to the lord's Steward.

One Sunday after church, the weary Priest sat heavily on a wooden bench.

"John, I think it is time I gave up some of my land. You have helped me often and I think I should talk to the Reeve about passing some of the land to you. I have more than I can manage, and you have a young family to feed. Most of it will be needed for the next priest, but there is some I took up a few years ago and I don't need it now. It has become a burden and a worry to me."

John was elated to hear this but made a manful effort to control his reaction.

"Twill feed the childern, to be sure. They be getting bigger and ungrier every day it do seem."

"I hope it will allow you to continue to support the church, John."

"Oh, ah," he replied.

Whenever land changed hands on the estate an entry payment was demanded; fortunately, John had a promising young steer available as a payment to their lord, the distant landowner. The deal was first agreed with the Reeve but had to be approved by the Steward and agreed in the manor court.

John had hoped the young steer would be sufficient, but the Reeve disagreed,

"Ee won't be ready for another year."

"Ah but look at im. Look at his back, an ee got all is life in front of im."

The Reeve persisted, "They wunt av it, they wunt ave it. I've aseen it before. You be getting it for three lives mind."

"Oh, ah, but zum of they lives might be short."

"Well, if you don't want it someone else'll av it."

John was silent knowing the Reeve was right. This might be his only chance.

"Awright, awright, four bushels of wheat then."

"No, a quarter twill av to be, fer they to take it."

"Oh, awright then, an a dozen eggs fer thee."

The Reeve turned slowly towards John, his face like stone, who responded quickly, "Two dozen then, but thass all I got."

The Priest's land allowed them to grow more wheat though their six children were big eaters and there were few seasons when wheat could be sold. Innate caution reinforced by the barren seasons in John's youth, made him very insecure and he rationed the use of grain with extreme care. He preferred to be using grain from the previous harvest at least till September, a target which secured a margin of safety.

In north Wiltshire an abundance of woodland grazing enabled the villager already blessed with a modest amount of land, an opportunity to develop herds of cattle and flocks of sheep. In the wet years there had been plenty of grass and weeds for the cattle to eat, though in a dry year some very thin cattle were tethered on any space carrying a few green leaves. Jealousy and protection of the villager's own rights led to fierce quarrels, sometimes violence.

The single cow that John had inherited from his father had, over a period of ten years, produced two daughters and a granddaughter. These were known to the children as Primrose, Bluebell and Lightfoot, but seemed not to respond to their names. Still, they served as family pets, though no child was in any doubt that they might be needed for the table at some point.

Edith and Edwin were already working a full day; Wilfrid and Juliana, like all children, absorbed and copied the daily influences around them and little Morris imitated them as they had once imitated Edith and Edwin. They all joined in when the cattle were taken to some common grazing near the river early in the morning. The cattle knew the routine and allowed themselves to be led to the place they wanted to go to. Anything the cattle could graze at the roadside was free food and the children knew it. Frequent stops and starts prolonged the journey and it might easily be two hours before they returned to the farm. Provided they each brought home an armful of firewood John did not complain about the delay. Late in the day the cows were brought back with their sucking calves which were then separated overnight; hungry young calves and anxious cows bleated and bellowed through the night till Joan and the older girls came out of the house to milk them.

Baby Hilda was not strong, and Joan was careful and protective. When Hilda eventually managed to walk, she would not venture far from her mother and never enjoyed the rough and tumble of her elder sisters and brothers. Nor was she expected to help with the rough animals though did become a careful dressmaker.

The extra milk they produced was made into cheese which was stored inside the thatched house for several months before it could be sold. Space was increasingly cramped inside the house; tensions grew within the family to Joan's sorrow, most notably between Edwin and his father. They had all heard the tales of their father who had managed the little farm early in life, and Edwin had perhaps assumed that some land might be passed to him at an early age. But John was a grim survivor who clung hard to everything he had gathered, moreover he had younger children to raise also. Conversation between the two, never fluent, had broken down; brief irritable exchanges were separated by long silences.

After some skilful prodding by Joan, John accepted the need to increase their accommodation. The house was extended by a permanent structure separated from the existing house by an open passage, this only joined to the house much later when re-roofing became necessary. Good timber for the frame of this building was secured from nearby woodland at a price agreed with the Steward but augmented by fallen waste when the Steward had left the village. Edwin became quite skilful at cutting the joints and helped his father to construct the trusses.

The main timber posts had to be set up on stone footings to ensure a long life, and stone was in short supply in this district. A derelict building on the estate produced a small amount of stone in return for two days unpaid labour. John enquired for scrap stone at the quarries in Calne, but the cost was too high. The difficulty of transporting heavy stone from Calne was also an obstacle.

He thought he might find some stone on the Marlborough Downs for nothing, so one day after milking he took Edith and Edwin with two of the cows hitched to the sled. When they returned very late in the day, they encountered an irritable wife and mother who had looked after all the young children, made the cheese and done the evening milking. Edith was desperately tired, but she immediately bustled around to help her mother get the evening meal and discretely nudged Edwin to help out.

The thatched roof was made from wheat straw they had grown on their own land, combed by hand and straightened into helms that could easily be laid on the roof without disturbing the straw. Over the course of many months hazel wands were interwoven to form the walls then plastered with a mix of clay and lime.

By chance, this instinctively practical design was a reasonably good imitation of the long houses with a cross passage separating animals from family, already found on some manor farms. A simple loft was then constructed on stout supports while the original house with its open fire remained as single storey, wood smoke finding its own way through the thatch. Maturing cheese could now be stored in the loft beneath the roof and there was room for Edwin and Wilfrid to sleep between the cheese racks; cattle were housed on the ground floor providing warmth and a priceless supply of manure for their own crops.

The cost of the timber was substantial, but the use of coin was growing amongst the more prosperous villagers and while John's farm was not yet very large, his cheese sales were bringing in regular sums of cash.

Edith was the first to marry, to a young man whose father and brothers farmed at Compton a few miles away on a small estate close to Calne. The family, like most farming families, had a scatter of arable strips in the common field, and grazed a few sheep on the common. A common grumble among sheep farmers was the declining price of wool, "Never like this in my father's day." And the price of wool had fallen with a decline in raw wool exports. Lower prices, however, encouraged an export growth in woollen cloth, centred on Salisbury, sending out through the port of Southampton.

Edith soon started milking some of the sheep to make a different kind of cheese and these cheeses she took into Calne market for sale. She came to enjoy the bustle of the day and the company of visiting villagers, including sometimes Edwin and more rarely her quietly spoken mother. In later years the two-hour walk from White Clyffe carrying eggs or apples became too much for Joan and she handed the marketing function over to the younger children.

Edwin worked on the farm with dwindling enthusiasm, though his boyish younger brothers were still quite happy working for their father. Much of the year was spent ploughing the great open fields, often three or four separate teams of eight beasts could be seen moving very slowly from horizon to horizon. Generally ploughing was done by strong young men with reserves of stamina allowing them to keep trudging through sticky ground for hour upon hour.

A daily record was kept of whose strip of land was being ploughed, who provided the cattle and the plough and who worked the plough and for how long. The farmer or smallholder would have obligations to all of the people who contributed to the co-operative effort, and though this obligation might be recorded in shillings and pence, it might be discharged variously by cash, grain or hours of labour. Few people could read or write so memories could be put to a severe test requiring the debt to be cleared within a few days; grumbles and arguments were a normal feature of the co-operative method.

Edwin already in his twenties could see no chance of getting a farm till his father died and no prospect of marriage and a life of his own. Alone of the children, Edwin rebelled against his cautious strong-willed father and perhaps fired by childhood tales of the wonders of Salisbury, eventually left the farm and never returned. Edith took this very hard and even years later, with children of her own, still grieved for her lost brother.

Edwin first left the farm to work in Calne, and Edith sometimes managed to see him when she visited Calne market. After about a year, at a time when work was short in Calne, he walked to Salisbury with two friends, one of whom subsequently returned to Calne; they had worked together in a weaving shop called Toomers, but the friend could not bear the dreadful din which left him exhausted each day. Edith had taken some eggs and whey butter to sell in the weekly market and by chance had got into conversation with Edwin's friend; she was thrilled to get news of Edwin, and always found time to chat when they met again.

CHAPTER FIVE

Alice and the Steward.

Those who survived the famine enjoyed a period of relative stability and though foul weather caused short-term problems, nothing again matched the devastation. From his endless travels the Steward knew of severe storms and flooding causing damage and loss on the Somerset Levels for example. Everyone in south Wiltshire remembered a succession of floods on the Avon below Salisbury. He also knew that poor land in Hampshire suffered from declining crop yields and there were rumours that whole villages had walked away from cultivated land on Dartmoor. But most of Wiltshire had survived, even recovered in the last twenty years of his life.

The Steward's normal routine was to return to White Clyffe at least every three months and Alice was now employed to manage and maintain the big house. The house resembled a small, thatched, tithe barn and it had replaced an earlier house that had burnt down when a fire in the kitchen got out of control and destroyed everything in a couple of hours. This replacement house originally had a detached kitchen to reduce the risk, but gradually the owners came to stay less and less, and the hall had not been used for grand dinners for at least fifty years. The house was now used for the management of the estate by a succession of Stewards on their infrequent visits; it had become more convenient to use the big fireplace in the hall for cooking and eating.

Food storage had long been a problem and the pantry had to be cleaned out thoroughly while the house was empty. Alice pointed out that this was wasteful, and if she lived in the house it would be better stocked and there would be a warm fire to welcome the Steward when he arrived.

The Steward recognised the advantages of this arrangement quite quickly, perhaps because they were lying together when she first raised the subject. He began to find good reasons to stay here even when visiting other estates in the district and this happy arrangement continued for quite a few years.

Alice had worked her way through the old house and had found a tester bed in one of the chambers which she cleaned up and stained the woodwork anew. The bedding had probably not been used for a long time so that was washed and deloused thoroughly. The mattress was beyond use, so she emptied out the old feathers and burnt them, and when they had killed some geese for Christmas, she took the feathers for their new bed. And wasn't he pleased when she showed him her work one Saturday; so pleased that they spent almost the whole of Sunday in bed together. Somehow, he found a goose feather and he tickled her mercilessly; later she used the feather to revive his attention. He came to think that was the best Christmas he had ever enjoyed in his whole life.

Only the Reeve disliked the arrangement because his estate was now under closer scrutiny, but he also worked in the house quite frequently because his records had to be stored here. Though a confirmed bachelor, he was coming to enjoy the company of women and became noticeably more relaxed. However, he was discretely absent when the Steward made his visits.

But the Steward is aging, having fought in the Welsh Wars, and his battered body has become a burden to him. Eventually he becomes too old for the hard riding and depends more and more on his young men. In his final years he is based at White Clyffe, nursed by Alice; he had enjoyed many sexual affairs over the course of his life but had never married, though now was of a mind for stable companionship.

Alice and the aging Steward would ride together in the dog cart pulled by a single horse, travelling for several hours some days to the more distant estates, where he would hope to catch his young men slacking or a lazy Reeve sleeping behind a hayrick. He kept up a constant commentary as they travelled, delighting in the quality of a team of eight young steers ploughing on the manor farm, his manor farm, or grumbling when another team was being turned at the headland and the ploughman had stopped to clean the mud from his boots.

The villagers always seemed to be standing about talking to each other, moaning about the weather or the weak market for cheese he supposed. He may or may not have been aware that the villagers were becoming a bit more confident and less servile. He was sure they seemed less inclined to pretend to be working than they did when he was younger. Occasionally, in his travels, he might find a larger group of ten or a dozen people being addressed by a single person who he could not identify, and that troubled him. He knew the stamp of discontentment well enough from his time in the military.

Arriving at an estate that was being inspected he drove the cart straight up to his men and asked, "Where is the Reeve?"

The more senior one, a smartish young fellow who had been well drilled, though had never served under fire he suspected, stepped forward and said, "We have checked his figures and they tally quite well with the stock of threshed corn. Cattle numbers are down a bit and they are bringing in the sheep now."

"Well watch out for fly strike in this warmer weather. And how much wheat have they sold?"

"Ah, well, we have not got that far yet. This is our first day."

"We'll hold the court tomorrow, mind, so you'll need to get that sorted pretty quick."

"Sir!"

The Steward turned to Alice, "We'll have to stay here the night. Have a look around and see what they have got for us." He did not need to tell her to make sure it was comfortable and there was enough food for them all, though that had often been a problem over the years; a consequence of his surprise visits he would admit. And in those days, he did not mind his own hardship if he could keep them on their toes.

Alice enjoyed these journeys, especially the shorter journeys to Calne which took barely an hour by a trotting horse, travelling through Hilmarton and the tiny settlement at Beversbrook. More than once the Steward told her the story of Nigel the Doctor, a court favourite, who had been given this land by the good Old Saxon king, at a time when Calne often received visits from the Kings of Wessex and their council of advisors.

At times he had to be away for weeks on business to the outlying estates, or was called to visit the owners in London, a punishing journey at his age. Alice remained at White Clyffe and kept the house in good order ready for his return. The Reeve was visibly more cheerful during these absences and seemed to find it necessary to bring some work to the house most days. He often lingered by the big fire in the hall; sometimes she wondered if he was lonely, he seemed to have few close friends in the village.

When the Steward returned, usually exhausted, she would help him out of his heavy boots and topcoat and lift his feet up on cushions; often he would be asleep before she could bring him his beer. The fierce old Steward had vanished, and she would let no one see him in this state.

Sometimes when he came to his bed, he would stroke the smooth woodwork of the tester bed which reminded him of his mother's bed in Hereford where he was born. His happiest memories of those years were when he was allowed into her bed on one side with his sisters on the other. His father had often been away, indeed had never been there on a regular basis at any time in his childhood; on military duties it was assumed.

Then there had been a funeral, friends and family gathered in sympathy. Two or three 'uncles' continued to visit with degrees of sympathy and support, one more persistent than the others. The boy began to resent the interloper and after his mother remarried, he saw his childhood had ended; the army beckoned, and he left with few regrets.

Slightly startled he returned to the present, still holding the bed post. He responded to Alice with a tired but grateful smile and she slipped her warm arms around him with a gentle kiss.

His last years were a sad decline from a man of power. A young Steward had been appointed to take his place and he made considerable efforts to assist the new man in the early months when his health allowed. As he grew weaker the young man would sit by the fire after the main meal and would make an effort to find something to talk about.

Generally, the old boy only wanted to talk about the past and it could be quite difficult to extract essential information needed for the job in hand. The new Steward would eventually excuse himself as he had had a long day and would have to make an early start. Before he was out of earshot, a loud voice intended for Alice could be heard, "God, when I was his age I could drink and talk till midnight, with no trouble at all."

At his funeral in Calne, he was remembered with respect. The Priest and the new Steward performed their duties, but the Reeve looking around at the faces saw that only Alice was showing a sense of loss. He would have gone to her, if only he knew what to say or do.

Three years later the Black Death arrived in Wiltshire, cutting down one third of the population in a few months. The terror cannot be imagined. Many must have feared that everyone in the village would die. But in the village basic decencies survived; John, together with the Reeve and two or three others collected the dead bodies and arranged for their burial. A degree of normality was maintained. The old Priest had died before the plague and had not been replaced; John as an unofficial lay preacher had recited some useful phrases in Latin, which served till a visiting Priest could conduct a group service in the graveyard. During these months John lived in a building away from the house to protect Joan and the family from the risk of infection which he was sure he would catch.

But the greatest burden was carried by the Reeve. No one had been prepared; the people of White Clyffe would have to look after themselves. The young Steward had moved on to other estates, but no one knew where; everything fell to the Reeve. He called a meeting to be held at the big house. It was quite a small meeting; they had no Priest, so John would have to fill in as best he could. A few farmers and smallholders also attended.

There had been rumours for a year of this devastating pestilence spreading across Europe, though most people assumed it would not cross the water. When it did a few far-sighted people understood there would be extremely high mortality, and to some extent the Reeve was prepared.

For eighteen months the small group worked together and there were always people in and out of the big house. At first Alice, still wracked by grief, had to force herself to meet people but dealing with an overwhelming emergency enabled her to keep functioning and with almost everyone in the village losing someone, there was a companionship in sorrow.

The men, who collected the bodies and laid them on a flat cart to take them away, gradually developed a gallows humour that strengthened their bond in mutual support. And when someone in the group was down another person was there to help. Years later the active group were able to look back on these frantically busy years with deep satisfaction; a period when they carried this extra burden in addition to their normal daily work.

Approximately eighty burials took place in the village over a period of eighteen months, peaking in the warmer weeks of the year when there might be four or five buried side by side in any one week. But in the autumn of the second year the numbers declined till the cold weather came, when there were no more. The winter was a period of contemplation when exhausted and damaged people were relieved to have survived. The short days and long nights provided a period of natural rest that their bodies needed before lengthening days lifted them again. The younger people led the way and started work in the fields as soon as weather allowed.

The Reeve was beginning to think he should hand over his burden, but not till he had got things straight again. The whole village was a pretty pickle, and the fields were a disgrace. Alice continued to manage the big house, but often travelled to Calne in the dogcart for extra company; frequent visits to an ale house on the green at Calne led to new friendships.

One day the owner was short-handed and almost without thinking Alice started to help, clearing plates, and washing pots. The owner was darting back and forth to the kitchen and drinkers were impatient at the bar.

Alice took control, "Steady on now, don't injure yourselves. What will you have?"

"Wass think, missus. Jist fill en up, I be dying o' thirst ere."

She took his pot and filled it from the barrel and having already worked out the price, took his money and gave him his change. Others clamoured for a drink and she jollied them along, the shouting subsided and normal conversation resumed.

The owner looked around the door and saw she was coping so he left her to it. Two hours passed in a flash, people came and went and gradually the bar thinned out. She chatted easily when time permitted,

"You used to be on this side of the bar. How long have you been over there?"

"About three hours, I'd say."

The owner brought a plate of bread and cheese and offered some to the last customer, who declined.

"No, I must be gone. Goodnight to ee both."

The owner locked the door and they sat together at one of the cleaner tables.

"Tis far too late for you to go back to White Clyffe tonight. There is only one problem, all the rooms are taken."

Alice looked at him with a face of great innocence, "So, what can we do then?"

He puffed out his cheeks and breathed out slowly, "Well you can share anything I've got, if you've a mind."

"I'll just wipe off these tables before they stain."

"Well the hoss is alright for the night. Young Amos saw to im a while ago so no need to bother about that."

CHAPTER SIX

A Search for a Lost Brother.

A few years after the first plague had ended, after long sleepless nights wondering what had happened to her brother, Edith together with young Wilfrid and Edwin's friend walked to Salisbury and began to enquire for Edwin son of John. They found the weaving shop called Toomers where the owner remembered Edwin, but he had left to take a more responsible position with a larger business. Here losses had been heavy, and they were disappointed to find no-one who could help. By chance, news of the quest reached a former colleague who, after Edwin died, had found a piece of carved wood in a pocket of his working smock which said, 'Edwin son of John' and passed it to the church.

He visited the church in some haste that same day and spoke to the Priest. "There are people in the city looking for Edwin son of John, who worked with me, but he died in the plague. He carried his name with him, and I handed it to the church a year ago. Do you think we could find it now?"

The Priest was sympathetic, "There is a box full of relics. We'll have a look."

After a lengthy rummage they found a small, dusty slice of fine-grained wood, which had once been polished, and dimly they made out the words 'Edwin son of John.' The former workmate wanted to take it, but the Priest said, "Edwin worshipped here, and his memento belongs here. But if you see them again, send them to me."

Returning at once to the deafening racket of the weaving shop where he once worked, he found the manager and by sign language conveyed a need to talk. They moved into the street where speech was possible, the manager removed a tuft of wool from one ear and listened intently with his head inclined towards the speaker.

Luckily Edith had told the manager they were lodging at a cheap inn just off Milford Street. Fearful they might already have left Edwin's friend went immediately to this address and found a woman and two men arguing in the road. Edith did not want to give up the search, but her brother felt they had been away from the farm too long.

Hesitantly, he approached them, and asked if they were the people searching for their brother. Edith turned to him, her face alive with hope, "Yes, yes, yes we are."

He replied, "I knew Edwin well and worked with him till he died. He carried his name in his overall and I gave it to the church."

Edith, "Oh, where is the church? Will you come with us?"

They found the church again and spoke to the Priest who confirmed that he had the little piece of carved wood, but the church would require a contribution.

Wilfrid said, "All we have is a penny and we have three days walk back to the farm, with no food."

The Priest replied, "Our lord fasted for longer than three days."

He took the coin and handed the carved wood to Edith. She gazed at it lovingly and two tears ran down her cheeks.

Wilfrid asked "Can we take it with us? Our father would like to see it."

But Edith said quite firmly, "No. It belongs here, where he worshipped."

The Priest replied, "Let us pray together for Edwin and to give thanks for your discovery."

The journey from Salisbury on an empty stomach was hard indeed and they chewed leaves and sucked pollen from flowering grasses to ease the pangs of hunger. Edith and Edwin's friend Judd were in high spirits together, often forgetting young Wilfrid who struggled to keep up. On the third day as they neared Calne, Edith turned away from the town to continue alone to Compton, but when she saw the desolate face of young Wilfrid, she knew they must all come back with her to eat and rest.

Her husband was rather reluctant to share her homecoming with his brother-in-law and a complete stranger, but Wilfrid by now was white and trembling with exhaustion, and there was really no alternative. Edith turned first to her two young children, then put some food on the table, which Wilfrid and Judd fell on ravenously, and were quite unable to talk to anyone; Edith was preoccupied with the babies. Her husband gazed at the scene, as a stranger at someone else's feast. He turned away and went outside, ostensibly to check the sheep.

Later Edith told her father how they found what had happened to Edwin; she thanked him for teaching them all how to read and write. Without his written name they would never have known where he was buried. A little gruffly, as he struggled to control his emotions and embarrassed by his weakness, he demanded that she do the same with her children.

After Edith had taken her children and set off for Compton, John and Joan sat quietly for some time. Softly he said "Well, Joan."

As one they rose to their feet, left the house and walked to the churchyard to visit Hilda's grave who they both missed quite badly. They had nursed her during her last days not many years earlier, when the plague was diminishing, and they were daring to hope their family might have escaped lightly.

A few days later John came down the ladder from the cheese loft and walked silently into the house. He cut himself a piece of bread and drew a mug of beer. Joan looked up from her sewing and said, "Been turning the cheese, then?"

Absently, John replied, "Yes."

"Everything all right John?"

"I was looking at the joints in the roof that Edwin and I made, all those years ago. Still as good as the day we did it. He was a good carpenter."

Joan remained silent but reflected that this was the first time he had mentioned Edwin since he left them to work in Calne.

Life had gradually returned to normal on the little farm though the house seemed strangely empty as it had when first Edith, followed soon after by Edwin, had moved away. Now there were only Wilfrid, Morris and Juliana and they were all busy with farming, cheesemaking and marketing. Juliana helped her mother at Calne market accompanied by one of the men when the winter evenings closed in; they would be carrying produce in the early morning, but even more tempting, they were carrying cash home in the dark and must have a man to protect them. As far as possible, the small farmers travelled together for security, but even in a group they required some men on dark winter evenings.

The sharp decline in population across the entire country reduced the demand for food and market prices fell at Calne market also at Chippenham and

Devizes. There had been a gradual, if erratic improvement in prosperity in earlier years, but this now declined.

However, a family of working farmers could carry on with very small purchases. The rent continued as before and the lords resisted all attempts to reduce this, expecting that life should continue as normal. But idle land in the common arable fields and empty houses brought the lord no income. Also, the production from their own manor farm had fallen sharply while still paying the surviving villagers either with grain or coin. Reluctantly the estates had to offer the uncultivated land at lower prices to tempt the villagers.

Some extra acres were offered to John at a low price in an attempt to keep him making his existing payments. John did not dismiss this offer but opened a discussion with the Steward for a formerly independent farm that had been empty for some years since an unmarried farmer had died there in 1348. The house was badly neglected and the land at that end of the village was poorly drained and difficult to cultivate. John suggested that an area of about ten acres should be fenced off from the common fields and grassed down and let to Wilfrid, together with a share of the arable strips in the common fields as before; the Steward heard this in silence, but returned to White Clyffe only a month later with instructions.

For John and his family this was a considerable investment in the future at a time of lower incomes from cheese and wheat and all produce. The Estate provided seed and breeding livestock on the ancient basis retaining a claim on production for the term of Wilfrid's life. Juliana joined Wilfrid to manage all aspects of the new farm, but both continued to live in the family home till the house could be improved.

These arrangements were repeated throughout the village, and many other villages. Within about fifteen years only the best soils in the common fields were still being cultivated while the poorest land had been converted to grass closes and farmed with sheep or cows. The Steward also instigated a similar arrangement on part of the manor farm. The shift from open field cropping land to enclosed dairy and sheep farms was now under way on many heavy land manors across north Wiltshire.

Both John and Joan were over fifty years old now and considered quite ancient, though John's brain was as sharp as ever and he followed the management of the farms with interest. It was becoming clear that there were advantages for the villagers following the massive reduction in population; for the first time in John's life there was land available. Though the labour obligations were still enforced, payments were increasingly made in cash and villagers at all levels were gaining a sense of independence. A new generation had rising hopes and expectations and a few villagers found the feudal stranglehold irksome.

CHAPTER SEVEN

Edith the Market Trader.

Edith had returned from Salisbury at peace, now she knew the circumstances of Edwin's death. Though her husband seemed not to be aware of either her former anxieties or her new contentment.

The next morning, she settled down to milking the sheep, singing gently as the milk flowed freely and making a satisfactory froth in her wooden bucket. She had missed two market days in Calne and needed to get back to work, so threw herself into her work with vigour making cheese and selling the surplus in Calne market. When they were not needed for farm jobs, she took two oxen and the heavy oxcart to market, which allowed her to carry two or three heavy cheeses. Judd, who lived in Calne was a great help, and stored the unsold stock of cheese in his house. At other times she had to walk to Calne and could only sell the eggs or butter she was able to carry.

Judd knew an old woman in the town who kept a pony that had belonged to her husband. Since he died the pony had not been used and the work of feeding and mucking out the pony was becoming a burden, though the manure was a treasure. Judd helped the old woman with the heavier work, and she came to trust him. One day, when she grumbled about the pony, Judd suggested she might try to sell and if she wanted him to find a buyer he would try to help. Judd had mentioned the pony to Edith months before, but the courtship of the owner required time; perhaps now she would sell willingly. After a couple of weeks, he brought Edith to see the pony and to meet the old lady. Edith's diminutive height touched the old lady and her story of only being able to carry a few eggs to sell in the market aroused sympathy. Nevertheless, the owner asked a hard price and Edith was disappointed, for she had been dreaming of owning her own pony for several months.

"That is more than I can manage. Can you see your way to letting it go a bit more reasonable?"

"Twere my dear husband's delight, that little pony, and it is all I have to remember him by."

Now it was Edith's turn to feel sorry for the seller. "I'll go back to the farm and see what they say."

Two weeks later Edith and Judd returned to the old lady, and after a suitable period of admiring the pony and rubbing her nose, Edith raised the thorny topic again.

"Have you thought any more about selling?"

"Well, she is getting on a bit in years, like me, so I can come down a bit."

The figure she mentioned was still more than Edith could find; after considerable reflection Edith said she could only pay half of that, but if the pony lived a year, she would pay another shilling. Eventually they agreed to a second shilling after a further five years if it included the rickety old cart, and if the pony was still alive.

Her business grew steadily over a period of time, and she was away from the farm more and more, often taking her small children with her. Her husband meanwhile was also working long hours, but his strength was declining. Work that he could once accomplish easily had become a hard slog. Still, at the end of a long day he could at least relax with lifelong friends who were dealing with similar frustrations, though none had an independent wife who seemed to have no need of a husband.

Two more children were born over the next four years, but the older children were maturing quickly; expecting little they were rarely disappointed. They helped their mother bring in the sheep for milking, and after the morning milking they loved to let the lambs go back to their mothers, tails wagging furiously as they pummelled the ewes for milk. However, collecting eggs from aggressive and broody and furious hens was a testing adventure they only gradually grew to enjoy.

As weeks and months passed their horizons extended beyond the familiar safety of the home paddock. Bees never buzzed so loud nor buttercups bloomed so yellow again as they did on those first adventures. Walking the ewes and their lambs to their pasture with their mother was a daily delight soon after sunrise.

But on market day, once a week, this was done briskly, and the ewes were not allowed to linger. The family hurried back to the house as fast as their little legs would permit, then once cleaned and washed and dressed for wind and rain, they were lifted into the cart beside all the market goods. The little ones were usually dropped off with Edith's sister-in-law before she hurried off for Calne. The journey from Compton lasted almost an hour but was relieved by the first food of the day, newly baked bread and homemade whey butter.

Edith was eternally busy with her children and the market business but was soon distracted by the declining health of her father and mother. Morris, his wife, and young family were running the old farm and needed to operate from the farmhouse. When first married they had lived in an abandoned house along the village street only fifty yards from the farm, but as John grew frail, he and Joan moved in with Juliana and Wilfrid. This was too far from the old farm for John to reach so he was not reminded of farm jobs that he should fix but was no longer able to tackle. Wilfrid was a patient and untroubled son who sometimes took John for a slow walk on a fine day. John could never resist giving advice to anyone and Wilfrid listened amiably enough, nodding in apparent agreement, while lost in his own thoughts. Sometimes John sensed his inattention and rebuked him, though with no obvious effect.

Juliana was quick and smart, and Joan was a little overawed by her daughter. However, Joan was active enough to make herself useful in the house and was often left alone when Juliana was busy assisting the new Priest. He was settling in and though he had been in the village for two years, he was still in effect a stranger; he needed Juliana's practical help and local knowledge.

John got out of the house most days and made himself useful, sometimes staying out too long, coming in cold and wet to a chorus of anxious criticism. He would sit close beside the fire till steam rose from his saturated clothes; his cough grew worse and he seemed unable to shake it off. One day he did not get out of bed at the usual time and did not want anything to eat. As darkness fell his eyes closed and he never spoke again; by next morning his body was quite cold.

His death was accepted. Death was natural; life was natural. He had lived a long time, for more than fifty years and few had outlived him. Most of the village came to pay their respects and to cheer his family. He had served the church since a child and comforted every family at one time or another through many crises and times of fear; no one was more respected than this poor boy who had made his own way.

Joan survived him for several years, caring for Wilfrid, a kind and gentle man sharing some of her characteristics and natural reticence. Juliana was spending more and more time with the Priest, the Steward, and the management of the village. Joan effectively ran the household in Juliana's absence, though she needed more periods of rest to get through the day.

Most Sundays, Joan and Juliana tended John's grave, taking away the wilted flowers and adding fresh ones. One day in late May, on a soft and gentle day with a light breeze from the west, they lingered a while. Joan reflected on their life together.

"We travelled a long way from those early days. We hardly knew when we would eat again and if he had not called in with summat for us we could have starved. Ee were always good like that."

Juliana had become involved with village life during the plague years of 1348 and 1349; she had remained busy since, gaining confidence as she gained experience. She also helped the young Steward on his regular visits and twice a year there were extra preparations for the manor court. In compensation for the unpaid work, some extra arable strips had been added to the farm and Juliana's name had been added to the copyhold agreement.

The extra ploughing and sowing and weeding became too much for Wilfrid and they had employed a lad from the cottages further down the street. He seemed quite a quick lad and had a practical farming background as did most of the villagers, though was not accustomed to working six full days a week. He was small and skinny and too young to have grown muscles. Wilfrid saw that he was really only strong enough to work half days. The boy was extremely disappointed to receive only half the pay at the end of the first week but was told that when they started to cut hay in June he would have to work the full day and would be paid double.

The jingle of coins in his pocket was like music to a young boy. This was the modern world, and money meant freedom to agree his own terms and to change his master. The older generation already broken to unpaid day labour on the lord's terms, that may not have changed for a century or more, were more cautious.

"Don't get too cocky, son. You can stay in my house and work for any farmer, I s'pose. But when you want a house of your own what will you do?"

During haymaking and harvest the boy went home exhausted but his enthusiasm was sustained by thoughts of the large amounts of money that would be coming to him. Later he was back on reduced hours; when he turned up at all. He was soon searching for better paid work and longer hours, but most farms were busy at the same time and quiet at the same time. There was plenty of threshing throughout the winter, but he had no experience and would not acquire the basic skills without months of practice. Inevitably, he was drawn to Calne where he found menial work earning better money than anything available in the village.

Wilfrid did not need to replace the lad till things got busy again in the spring. He returned to the same family taking a younger brother, though within the year this lad had also followed his brother to Calne. Later, Wilfrid was approached by a boy with no father, who had to care for his mother and the younger children. He was a steady lad mature beyond his years and Wilfrid took to him immediately. Over the years their relationship ripened to a form of friendship. As time passed Joan needed more help in the house putting an extra burden on Juliana who was always in demand somewhere in the village, so it was natural to offer a few hours work to the boy's mother. Eventually Joan's health declined and for several months she became more dependent on Edith and Morris for support; she survived the winter and lingered till the start of haymaking in June when the flowers were in full bloom.

Meanwhile at Compton, Edith's husband grew resentful of her busy life and responsibilities, often returning tired at the end of the day to a cold and empty house. Sometimes he collected the children from his brother's house where they had been happy with their cousins and were reluctant to leave for their own bleak home. But increasingly he leaves them for Edith to collect, preferring the company at the alehouse, returning reluctantly and late. After another long day at the market Edith developed the ability to feign sleep quite convincingly.

The declining days of October and November were dispiriting enough to busy ambitious people, but her husband was a lost soul and was gradually losing control of his drinking. He would delay his return as long as possible, even on the days when she did not attend a market; on some nights he did not return at all. Increasingly, his brothers would find him sleeping beside a hayrick and not at all grateful for being woken.

After some months of this erratic behaviour, it was no longer a surprise that he had not been seen anywhere around the farm. Edith was loading her cart with goods and produce as she did on all market days; she made off for Chippenham with all the children, the eldest helping their mother while the little ones playing pretend games around the market stall. Edith was reassured to have them all together, and it was almost as if she feared the worst.

Returning unusually early from market she went to see her brothers-in-law, "Have you seen him?"

"Bain't seen no sign nowhere."

"Well ask at the alehouse to see if he was there last night, and when he left."

When she returned to her little house, the children had unloaded the cart, rubbed the horse down, fed and watered her and left her for the night. The fire was lit already, and she sat for a few minutes hugging the children.

"Did you find Dad?"

"No Uncle Ellis, and Uncle Gilbert, have gone out to look for him again. Tomorrow we'll search a bit further. We'll have more time than today."

But they found nothing that day, nor the next. The realisation grew in all their minds that they were not going to see him again. Edith drew them close; their aunts, uncles and cousins also did their best to be bright and cheerful around the little ones.

Days became weeks, time passed, spring approached, and heavy rains were too much for swollen rivers. The Avon at Chippenham and Melksham rises quickly, flooding broad areas of meadow land. For two days a brown torrent carried trees and dead cattle at high speed, smashing everything in its path like a furious and implacable god. But this river goes down as quickly as it rises. Word came of a body, common enough after a flood, but the uncles went to see if it was their brother. It was about the right height and build but they could not identify him with certainty, and it had been many months since he was last seen. Edith clung to the hope that he was alive somewhere and felt sure they would know him when they saw him.

For the family, hard work and a regular routine was the only comfort. They just got their heads down and carried on. For Edith, caring for her children and driving her business to provide them with a long-term security was her motivation. If she ever felt a weakness it was carefully concealed, though gentle Judd was not deceived. He helped her faithfully at market, even to the extent of neglecting his own market stall.

The wounds healed, humour returned, and her spirits lifted. Over the course of time, she could remember the children's father and smile at some of the memories; the healing had begun. She was grateful to her brothers-in-law, but they could not support a third family if only two men were working. Her eldest son could help with the lighter work but was not yet strong enough for heavy labour. She decided to attend more markets and to pay the family for the grain she needed and for the ewe's milk she used for cheese making. Already accustomed to travelling to Chippenham market when she had extra goods to sell, she now decided to sell at Devizes; three market days a week would make a big difference.

Judd was slightly concerned, "Tidden right fer you to be getting about on yer own."

"Oh, don't you worry, I'll be awright."

"I do worry. Better if I come along too."

Edith smiled her thanks. It was sensible, as she often had some of the children with her and would be glad of the protection. "We could sell some of your stuff on the same stall; though we'll have to buy in more to keep going three days a week."

Devizes was a new town, like Salisbury, and had only grown up around the building of the castle where the Normans had chosen a defendable site looking southwest across the Avon Vale. Semi-circular ditches had been dug across level ground on the eastern and northern sides, and these had restricted the development of the town. St John's Church had been built within the inner ditch but most of the space was still open; the church had managed a market within this area for many years. Beyond the inner ditch a second church, St Marys, served the town and was attempting to establish an independent market held on a Monday, but this was still a small affair. Established traders in Devizes used it to shift their leftovers from the main market.

Edith thought she must attend the 'old market' near the castle. The district administration was based at the castle and had replaced Calne two centuries before when the new rulers had established a huge stone castle surrounding a keep. This had replaced a temporary wooden affair that had burnt down within a few years. There were military people everywhere and even the serving staff had a sense of importance. On the other hand, the working people seemed to lack confidence and carried a respectful air of deference; they walked with a slightly hunched look, their heads drawn forward looking downward at the ground, only squinting at Edith out of the corner of their eyes.

The contrast with Calne was marked. Calne was still a Saxon town to its bones and the townspeople knew their worth. The stories of regular visits by the Saxon Kings and the Witan, the King's advisory council, were well known. Calne people had a strut, a vigour and a pride, which was quite lacking in Devizes. But it had to be admitted Devizes had money. The administration of the district was a source of wealth that trickled down and fed the town. There were some fine houses here and most of the smaller houses were in good repair.

Edith's basic supplies of cheese, bacon, homespun wool, and a limited range of woollen goods sold well enough. But her sons wondered if there might be a market here for better quality. Edith had enough vision to listen to her sons and began to wonder where she might buy better materials. She was alert for signs of wealthy houses clearing out their unwanted furniture and draperies and was smart enough to offer to clear everything at a bulk price to make it easier for the seller. Over time she built up a friendship with the housekeepers of better houses to their mutual advantage.

Travelling tinkers sometimes picked up fine woollens in Salisbury where a large manufacturing industry had grown up, and she hoped if time permitted, she might be able to visit Salisbury and buy direct at lower prices. Perhaps when the boys were older and were able to manage the business alone.

Edith had grown close to Judd and depended on his gentle, caring heart; he was such a steady comfort. Sometimes the boys took the wagon back to the farm while she remained in Calne with Judd to arrange business. The boys would spend the day off between markets buying cheese and wool from the farms further out from Calne, often contriving to stop at White Clyffe to see their cousins and uncles. Their uncle Wilfrid, still a bachelor living with his sister Juliana, was careful and frugal but kindly enough. They sometimes bought a little cheese, though it had to be mature and ready to sell; they needed to get their cash back in a few days. It was not at all uncommon to buy a single cheese, sell it over the next week and return to buy another cheese.

Visits to Uncle Morris were jollier events in a house full of younger cousins and their uncle took an intelligent interest in the marketing business. His herd of cows was growing, and he had a large cheese loft attached to the house, the old house where John and Joan had spent their lives. Sometimes when they had arrived in daylight, the family would walk together to the churchyard to see the graves and cut the grass. A bunch of fresh picked wildflowers would be left to decorate the grave. Aunt Juliana was developing into an expert flower gardener with a view to growing flowers for the grave beyond the wildflower season. She also used a small corner of the garden to bring on decorative plants for Christmas, a revolutionary step when people depended on the garden for winter food supplies.

One sunny day in January Edith was returning to the market area in Calne, when she saw an extraordinary man, very tall with a penetrating gaze. His eyes filled his face, the eyeballs were jet black and when he stared at her she was filled with a mixture of fear and exhilaration. He turned away and she followed him without a thought. He moved quickly, she scampered urgently on short legs, but as he reached the top of the church steps, he turned towards her again, and waited while she approached. Though the church steps were in deep shade the frost seemed to gleam with the reflected light from his personality. He turned away again; when Edith had climbed the steps and entered the church the Priest was already praying at the altar. She kneeled in the body of the church and prayed silently. At length, the Wandering Priest rose to his feet and walked towards Edith, pausing to lay his hand on her hair, very softly. As he removed his hand the fingertips brushed her hair along its full length.

Somewhat unsteadily she made her way back to the market on the green beyond the church, where Judd had cleared the stall and re-loaded the cart. He looked up as she approached, "Where have you been?"

"To Church" she replied and slipped her arm through his. "Can we go back to your place for a bit?" Judd responded with a slow smile.

An hour later, lying together in his bed in a limp and languid state, he said, "You ought to go to Church more often."

Edith laughed a laugh of pure love that sounded to Judd like a peal of tinkling bells.

CHAPTER EIGHT

The Village Reeve.

The catastrophic collapse in population was the catalyst for a succession of changes that led in time to a social revolution. The feudal system had been working successfully for at least six hundred years. The prime function was to put powerful armies into the field equipped with a dominant cavalry, secondly to manage the government of a large and complex kingdom.

The demands of the cavalry in particular, could only be met by a large group of wealthy knights, able to maintain a stable of fast powerful horses strong enough to carry a knight in full armour. The knight had to provide his own support teams, armour, and weapons and, at least while a young man, must be able to fight for months at a time and to maintain his training at other times. This could only be achieved by the ownership of a substantial estate.

The agricultural estates were therefore organised to provide the knight with everything he needed to fulfil his military duties. Over the centuries control of the kingdom had tightened, and in this century, long campaigns against the Scots and the French had cost far more than could be provided by traditional means. Taxation of wool exports now generated an income equal to the whole of English village agriculture, and this was still not enough. Direct taxation of movable goods owned by the wealthiest, including the church, sometimes at the rate of one tenth even occasionally of one fifteenth, topped up the supply of funds needed by the king to fight his wars.

The management of the rural estates was set in the tradition of bygone centuries and depended on free village labour managed by the Reeve, also a villager but often a lonely and isolated one. At White Clyffe the Reeve was already the largest farmer in the village and had followed his father into the role.

His nephew Wilmot had been involved with the daily routine of the farm for several years and this allowed the Reeve to concentrate on the management of the direct farming on the manor farm. He considered the management of the unwilling farmers and listless cottagers to be far more challenging than running his own farming business.

Frequently he had reminded the old Steward of the inefficiencies of the system and had obtained an improvement in the terms for his own farm to compensate for his time and frustration. He was convinced that specific labour obligations should be replaced by cash payment and the workers should have the choice of working fixed hours at the price on offer. But the ruling family were still rather conservative and having little contact with their agricultural estates did not fully grasp the need for change.

He had paid the workers weekly on his own farm for some years and knew the cottagers as wage earners came willingly to collect their money, if they came at all, and would be paid at the rate of 2d per day or one shilling per week. From experience he had learned to pay on the Monday of the next week, so when they were paid, they were still one day behind, and this encouraged them to turn up for another week. Wheat at 5 shillings per quarter was also accepted as currency and a good defence against inflation, at least while prices were rising. Though there was a limit to how much wheat a family could consume in a week.

The sharp loss of population in White Clyffe, and indeed the entire country, reduced the demand for grain purchases. More immediately there was an acute lack of men to plough the land and sow the seed. As a result, about one third of the great fields had not been planted for at least three years after the plague. In general, the worst land was left to grow weeds, but this led to a major re-juggling of the allocation of arable strips.

For years, the balanced arrangements had rarely needed a change so in 1348 and 1349 chaos reigned;

people were dying from the plague so frequently that any attempt to establish a planned reduction was immediately obsolete. Fortunately, there was now an abundance of wheat available to use as seed so the limited amount of land that had been ploughed was quickly planted with a new crop.

Maintaining a record was extremely difficult since the only person able to keep a comprehensive record, the old Priest, had died two years before the first wave of deaths and had not been replaced. The Reeve had a minimal grasp of writing, though a prodigious memory for detail. He had been assisted by John and especially John's daughter Juliana. Of these three Juliana adapted quickly as a young person always will and the Reeve came to depend heavily on her.

An awkward and clumsy man who had never married, the Reeve struggled to communicate the essential details without irritation. A request for clarification usually led to a repeated instruction in a louder voice. Juliana gradually learned that the most heated arguments about who had cropped which strip of land and how many hours of labour had been worked could usually be resolved by good humour and the possession of a mysterious written record. Over a period of months his confidence in her increased and the prickliness in his manner came to be replaced by a calm acceptance.

Most farmers and smallholders were hungry for land but when they had enough wheat for their own needs plus a reserve for insurance against famine, they were more interested in cattle and sheep.

A few landless cottagers managed to obtain a small amount of land satisfying a deep instinct as well as giving a sense of security for their family. Generally, there was now more arable land available in the villages of north-west Wiltshire than was needed; the estate soon calculated that the creation of little fields or closes to graze cattle or sheep would bring in more income.

The generation of plague survivors were more excited by the small flocks of wool producing sheep than the hard slog of ploughing, cultivating, sowing, weeding, and harvesting on soils that were not well suited to wheat growing. Most of the small farms of about thirty acres ran a few sheep in small paddocks of fenced land which they shared with no one. A few cows would be milked, usually in a paddock near the houses along the village street and a scatter of unfenced strips of land in the once great arable fields provided grain for their own use, perhaps a small surplus for sale after a good harvest.

Young Wilmot had quite a large flock of sheep, but most of the land coming available was more suitable for dairy farming and he rather missed the opportunity to develop a cheese making business, unlike John's two sons. As his uncle aged, Wilmot took on the duties of managing the day work on the lord's manor farm and this may have distracted him. Eventually his uncle moved out of the family home to live with his widowed sister and Wilmot set up again as another bachelor. But he was not voted in to be Reeve while his uncle lived, though for three years he had been doing the job in practice, if not in title.

During the years after 1350 the village population rallied till a second visit of the plague took a heavy toll of those born after the first plague and this became known as the plague of the infants; those who survived the first pestilence had perhaps gained a degree of immunity.

The second plague rattled many of the landowning class who had supposed things might return to normal. But the loss of a generation of children dashed those hopes and all but the dimmest recognised that the crop acres needed to be reduced to match the population. The lords were most reluctant to reduce rents, but they had to adjust to the new painful reality.

The villagers sensed the landowner's weakness and grew in confidence creating difficulties for Wilmot while still an inexperienced Reeve. Restlessness led to cussedness and perhaps even outright rudeness among the youngest, though usually kept in check by those who understood Wilmot's burden. The old Steward had been replaced even before Wilmot's uncle, but his replacement was not yet sure of his ground with the owners. However, like Wilmot and his uncle he understood the need to have willing people to work the manor farm. Slowly and diffidently he approached his masters to explain the difficulties. Some of the cropping land would have to be converted to grassland and an agreed value would be placed on a day's labour. On one day per week the cottagers would do their quota of unpaid employment without pay but would also be paid at the agreed daily rate for extra days.

The Reeve's role changed from being an organiser of quite a large group of working people to a recorder of attendance. The young Steward was aware of this and discussed the new fashion for leasing out the big farm at the centre of the estate, known in the village as the manor farm or the lord's farm. The principal member of the owning family had grown old, and though he could see the attractions of a predictable cash payment each year he felt it should be a decision for the next generation; perhaps thinking that paying peasants a cash wage was quite enough innovation for one lifetime.

A third wave of the plague after only eight years inflicted further pain on a bruised and battered generation. Any lingering hopes of a return to the old normal were dashed and the Steward was instructed to find suitable tenant farmers for the manor farms on each of the nine estates he managed. Not many people were able to contemplate taking on a large farm of several hundred acres but Wilmot the Reeve, who was already managing the labour at the Manor Farm had the confidence though not the financial means to do it. The estate supplied the plough teams and the equipment and the seed to crop 150 acres, together with a sum of cash to pay the wages through to harvest in return for an agreed share of the crop at harvest.

This was a considerable risk for Wilmot who would have been vulnerable in a bad season and must have lived with a feeling of anxiety for many months. In some other villages no one had been found willing to take the risk of failure and the process of change was slow and fitful. But gradually the old aristocratic families removed themselves from village life, and a new social level of large-scale tenant farmers emerged, alongside small farmers employing no labour. The cottagers became wage-earning labourers with the freedom to seek work in town or village. This was a gradual process throughout the country as a whole, but an abrupt revolution in a particular village, when it took place.

The change to payment of wages in cash was generally popular as it increased the freedom of choice, a freedom already enjoyed by workers in nearby towns. However, the replacement of the aristocratic lords of ancient tradition, by a villager in the manor farm left the poorer villagers with a sense of uncertainty. Would Wilmot carry the losses in a bad year? Could he keep paying the wages if some of his crops fail? And more than a whiff of inverse snobbery could be sensed in the phrase "Well, he ain't no gentleman and never will be."

A welcome and unexpected change slowly became evident in White Clyffe, as in much of the clay country of north Wiltshire, unwanted arable strips were fenced off into small fields and leased out to farmers and small holders in the village. At first the fences were made of timber and though stock-proof they required frequent repair after a few years. At the same time shrubs and small trees took root along the undisturbed fence line and farmers soon learned to bend young sapling growth and weave it into other existing plants to improve the fence. They quickly became aware that hawthorn was the most formidable barrier to sheep and cattle and planted this in any weak spot in the fence.

They had created living fences illustrating the biblical definition of the quick and the dead and hawthorn became known as quick thorn. The practical advantages of this technique were so obvious that it was taken up quite quickly across the country. The formerly bleak landscape of open arable blocks, with only a few windswept trees to break the monotony was replaced by an intricate patchwork of hedges seen at its most striking in undulating country.

After three years Wilmot began to feel more secure and bought himself a horse to widespread ribaldry, tinged with jealousy. "Now look how our new lord arises."

But Wilmot could now easily travel to other estates to visit other Reeves or newly appointed tenant farmers like himself. His isolation demanded the comfort of equal human contact, but perhaps in White Clyffe only his late uncle would have understood this.

CHAPTER NINE

A Wandering Priest.

His mother was a small but busy woman, like
Edith, who looked at him with a frank and open
face, as Edith also did in Calne a few years later. As
a child he was taken to his mother by her sister at
unpredictable intervals. She lived in a large house
with high ceilings and stone floors. His mother was
not alone in this house and people there moved
quietly about their work when he was taken to her.
She was always busy with her hands; her mind
engrossed in her work and was not permitted to
speak for this was a Silent Order. She stroked his
hair softly when he arrived and at greater length
when the time came to leave; these visits ended
before he reached puberty.

He was quite used to returning with his aunt to
an isolated house in pleasant grounds. His aunt did
not work. They were accustomed to living in a
certain style, though there were no visitors and
only a couple of quiet servants. As he grew older,
he became aware of a greater house within the
grounds, a busy house with people coming and

going. He knew he did not belong there and sensed he could not belong there, though it had been his aunt's home and must once have been the home of his mother, though he did not know why it was no longer so.

He explored the grounds and nearby farmyards and a small church where he often sat quietly watching sunlight streaming through stained glass, dust rising like a cloud of insects in coloured sunbeams. One day, and it must have been a Sunday, he followed a group of people into the church and was captivated by the Priest who controlled the whole dramatic event. In his solitude the boy lived in an imaginary world, vastly richer than his limited reality. For months he played the part of a Priest bringing the congregation to prayer, haranguing them with sermons of blood and fire, but kind-heartedly concluding with a couple of rousing hymns with a military flavour to send them away in a jolly frame of mind.

In the course of time, he was sent away to school where he was mildly brutalised, learned to avoid trouble and quite quickly developed the ability to manipulate his fellow pupils. In the second year he became increasingly bored and wandered out of the school grounds in quiet moments; he did not run away from school but returned in his own time. Explorations lasting a couple of hours were extended to take in distant hills and woods. Sometimes darkness overtook him, and he had to find somewhere comfortable to sleep. A few whacks with the cane on his return were a small price to pay for hours of freedom. Ever longer periods of detention were more irksome and only encouraged him to delay his return. An extended adventure led him to new villages and a town with a cathedral. He joined the congregation and threw himself into the responses. He was noticed by an older woman who asked him back to her house where she gave him a drink and offered him bread. He ate so much and so quickly that the kindly woman became alarmed.

His manners were good, he was well spoken but he was not at all clean; she quickly deduced that he had been sleeping rough. She gave him a bed for the night and in the morning took him to the Priest. The Priest suggested he continued his schooling with him while living with the kindly woman. He thrived in these conditions and in due course entered the church.

But again, he found discipline irksome, though continued with his studies and worked hard enough to make adequate progress. Eventually he obtained a post in Wells cathedral, but again his wanderlust caused problems. The Bishop in despair sent him to a large parish near Exmoor as a lowly assistant to the Priest.

He loved being alone on the open hills for a few hours, though was surprised to discover that he enjoyed company for a change, at least on his own terms. Finding a man working alone his curiosity prompted an excited stream of questions till the poor man was exhausted. The answers grew shorter and the man seemed often to need to walk away to pick up a tool or select a special stone. When his dog began to worry the sheep, the man moved with an energy that few would have foreseen, nor would have guessed at the telepathic understanding they shared.

The Priest's assistant watched them work the sheep for a moment then moved downhill towards the village. A small group of people standing by the alehouse caught his eye, he spoke briefly, one man recognised him and remembered his help of many months before. An awkward conversation developed, with his prompting. Soon he had them laughing, and the women in particular, responded to his instinctive warmth. It was only a matter of time before someone suggested it was time for a drink and naturally, he was drawn into the bar with the group. A few drinks and it was time to eat. He joined in with the collective meal with enthusiasm, entertaining them with practiced stories and opinions.

On some occasions they might grumble about their hardships and difficulties. His sympathy was genuine and his interest in their day-to-day problems not feigned; he genuinely sought to learn more of conditions he had never encountered. Usually, the villagers warmed to him and opened up freely. Over time he developed an understanding of the difficulties of feudal life in a deep rural district, a long way from Bridgewater and Taunton. It was a closed community with few if any opportunities or alternatives, except perhaps the sea. A purely agricultural village was completely controlled by landowners and the military aristocracy.

But the cloth trade was expanding in Somerset and mostly lay in the hands of a rising class of businessmen augmented, here and there, by an impoverished member of the gentry whose grandfather perhaps had owned an estate or two, but had passed nothing to the younger sons. Such a man was encountered on the road to Bridgewater. Three heavily laden wagons, each drawn by four oxen lumbering along a damaged road at two miles an hour was followed at a distance by a single man in a dog cart. He had followed his wagons for most of the day and was· bored, tired, and cold. Before him and kneeling beside a thorn, he saw a man in a soiled robe wiping his face with clean grass. The man trembled as he regained his feet, and his face was drained of all colour; he was clearly unwell.

The traveller brought his pony to a stop beside the shivering Priest and offered him a drink.

"Come, sit down," he said helping the frail figure into his cart. The gaunt face of the Priest was lit for a moment by a flash of gratitude from those dark unfathomable eyes. They moved off at walking speed, and a rather slow walk at that. When the priest was well, he would have overtaken the wagon train quite easily. The men were at ease together, though conversation was limited to pleasantries.

After a long hour, the teams ahead turned off the road into a yard surrounded by large storage buildings, all covered with thatched roofs. A timber framed house was attached to one of the workshops and the priest was led inside where they were met by a trim young woman.

"Jenny, help this man to a seat by the fire, he is not well. Ask the mistress to look after him."

"She is resting sir, but I can do it."

The Priest was taken into the hall where the fire had been burning the whole day. He sat down with relief and his spirits lifted as he felt the warmth spreading through his body. The maid brought him a large mug of boiling water with burnt crusts from the bread oven standing, or rather slowly collapsing, to make a flavoured soup. He managed a weak smile of thanks; her sympathetic heart was touched.

After a night's sleep he was somewhat improved, though still fragile. His gown had been washed overnight and had an unusually pleasant aroma. Later he thanked the mistress for her kindness though she seemed not to understand what he meant. Probably it was Jenny who had done it on her own initiative.

Later in the day when the sun broke through the clouds his spirit lifted sufficiently to take a stroll along the bank of a stream. Natural features in the landscape usually soothed his torments and nothing better than the gentle flow of clear water. He returned after an hour in better spirits. Jenny came across the yard from the house to the pump.

"Jenny did you wash my gown last night?"

"Yes Sir, you were sleeping so deeply I thought it better not to disturb you."

"Oh, I might not mind being disturbed by anyone as kind as you."

She dimpled prettily and seemed not at all displeased.

"Thank you Jenny I feel so much better in a clean gown."

"Will you eat with us tonight, Sir?"

"Yes, I think I will. I am feeling stronger."

The clothier was a model of courtesy and had clearly enjoyed a comfortable and reassuring childhood. His wife was brisk and conscientious but spoke little. When the Priest congratulated her on the spread of food on the table, she was modest in the manner of a comfortable farmer's daughter,

"It is no more than we are able to provide, sir."

She left an impression that her house was tightly managed.

Later he sat with the clothier by the fire. The Wandering Priest did not wish to press him closely, "I noticed your wagons were unusually robust"

"Of necessity, the roads here are poor and heavily used, like the village people."

His ironic smile deserved a response.

"Yes, I have seen hardship further west from here."

The conversation had not progressed much further before the clothier decided to test the Priest by stating, "The rural conditions are oppressive.

My own people owned land, so I criticise my own. The great lords take too much for their mighty households and extravagant pleasures."

The Priest replied, "I too have moved among the powerful."

"There must be change soon, and entered willingly, or we will see riot and retaliation; and blood will run assuredly."

The Priest sat quietly reflecting, gazing at the cheerful fire but feeling only despair at the clothier's understated forecast.

"But what can we do?"

"We must build a peaceful movement county by county and extend throughout the country. The poorer villagers will be overwhelmed by their own anger and resentment. Their riots will destroy their own villages and the military reaction will be vicious. Nothing will be achieved. Only calm reasonable talk will sow the seeds for change."

The Priest was lifted by his certainty and determination. He felt he could follow this man and could spread the vision of peace and progress through his own preaching.

"You inspire me sir. I share your dream. I will take your message, village by village and town by town."

The clothier was cheered by this response, "Yes, town by town, that is where we must start."

The Priest slept heavily and rose late. The hall was deserted, and he helped himself to some scraps of food. He walked slowly across the yard and though noises could be heard from some of the buildings he could find no people. It occurred to him it might be time for him to leave, and this would allow him to avoid those messy goodbyes and false sentiment. He wandered through the main gate and into the road, eastward he assumed, since the sun was in his face. His legs ached and he was unable to move at his usual speed but thought things might improve if he persevered. After about a mile he came to a ford where a strong flowing stream tumbled noisily over a rocky bed. Swaying weakly, he thought the rushing water would have him over, so he sat on a large stone hoping to regain strength, but only found the cold. Dragging himself to his feet he turned back to the clothier's yard making slow progress with frequent stops for rest.

He was seen by Jenny who knew at once he was exhausted as he saw him come towards the yard. She rushed to him and put her young arms around his skinny body.

"Oh, you are quite cold. You are not yet strong enough and must rest more often and stay warm. Come into the house and I will get the fire going. Everyone is away at Bridgewater Market so I have let it die down, but it will soon flare up."

Sitting in the chair in front of the dead fire he looked quite forlorn and she took a cold hand between her warm palms and attempted to rub some life into his extremities.

"Could you help me to my chamber, Jenny? If I lie down with a couple of rugs over me, I might recover."

Together they struggled to get his limp body to his bed, where she covered him with as much as she could find. His hands felt like ice and she rubbed them briskly but to little effect.

"I am so cold, and you are so warm Jenny. I wonder if you lay your warm body next to me it might help to make me feel better."

She lay down willingly and put her arms around his shivering shoulders for she was concerned that he might die. Her warmth seemed to comfort him in a strange way and his breathing became easier till he passed into a deep sleep.

When he awoke Jenny was standing over him with a bowl of steaming broth. "Do you know Jenny, I dreamed you were lying with me and holding my frail body."

"I was with you, but I am saying nothing and nor must you. Now get this inside you and that will do you more good."

He sipped slowly and she watched over him, wiping up the soup he spilt on his gown.

"You are a good kind girl, Jenny. You are a good girl, aren't you?"

"Oh of course sir, why would I not be?"

"I am afraid the sins of the flesh torment us all but promise me you will resist them to your utmost. You will, won't you?"

"Oh, I will indeed, sir."

"You must pray to be strong tonight before you go to bed. You do pray faithfully, don't you?"

"Oh yes sir, yes sir. I do."

"And do you find prayer a comfort, Jenny?"

"Yes, I suppose I do."

"Well I wish I did. I think perhaps there is no one listening, and I am all alone."

"Oh sir, you are not alone. We all care deeply for you."

"Yes, I think you do Jenny, and I am deeply touched. I don't suppose there is another bowl of good broth in your fine kitchen?"

The Priest realised he needed longer to recover his strength. The clothier also advised him to feed himself up for a few days before venturing forth. Unfortunately, there was a pressing need to attend the Tetbury wool sales, a long slow journey by oxcart. So, it may be many months before they could meet again but the Priest would always be welcome in his house, a sentiment not echoed by the clothier's wife.

The tender care from Jenny restored the Priest's spirits and he encouraged her to kneel beside his bed in prayer while he stroked her hair softly. The clothier's wife grew suspicious of these lengthy absences and one evening opened his door without warning. Her anxieties were only slightly mollified to find Jenny kneeling on the floor a little too close to the Priest for the reputation of a decent household; the next morning the Priest departed.

The clothier's wife was accustomed to the double burden of managing her household and the weaving shop in the yard, during long absences. The foreman came to the house mid-morning to discuss progress.

"We will have the cloth completed tomorrow, I think. Twenty- four yards long that be."

"So, you'll be foot-fulling for the rest of the week then."

"Yep. We are looking at the dam after the big bend in the stream, we'll want a lot of still water for this job."

"Got enough men?"

"Oh ah. If not, the weaver can get in the water and tread wi the rest of us, I daresay."

This prompted a smile; the weaver was known for his arrogance.

"It would be a fine sight, but it's more important to keep that big loom working."

The foreman nodded happily.

Two days later a chorus of shouting accompanied six or seven men and boys as they manhandled twenty-four yards of woven cloth out of the weaving shed, across the yard to the bank of the stream. The cloth was fed into the sluggish current, two people holding the other end secure. Four more men waded into the wide bend, most of them knee deep, ready to take the upper end of the cloth from the men on the bank. Fullers Earth was then rubbed into the first few yards of cloth before being trod repeatedly by four pairs of sturdy boots, the beginning of a long, repetitive, and tedious operation that would gradually cleanse the cloth and change its texture. A row of racks would allow the cloth to dry overnight before a repeat performance, for as many days as it might take. The wet and weary men were consoled by the thought of their wet money bonus, though this would not be paid till the cloth had passed the buyers test, many weeks ahead.

A year later, the Priest almost forgotten, Charles the clothier, meets with fellow businessmen in an alehouse in Bridgewater. They have discussed the wool market and the inadequacy of supplies and the unreliability of spinners and workers generally, as businessmen usually do.

Charles the clothier, suggested they have need to develop better contacts in Salisbury.

"The city is growing quickly and has valuable links with the port of Southampton."

"Are you thinking of exporting, Charles?"

"Yes, but not only France, which is disrupted by war too often. The low countries are more stable, and Southampton will get our goods into London quite quickly, which might be an easier market for west country cloth."

"All very true of course but we need better supplies from our own country. Tis a great muddle. A few sheep here, a few sheep there, and everywhere neglected and abandoned arable land that could carry hundreds of sheep." This comment came from a bright young man, a former pupil of Charles' who had set up with help from his family of ale-house keepers.

Charles was lost in thought, then quietly said, "We cannot allow the rural situation to drift. The villages are locked in the past, still cultivating the same ground when wheat was oversupplied. If farmers could enclose a few acres they would fill with sheep in no time; repeated across the country will bring in a great harvest of wool."

"Ah, but will they listen to anyone, ever."

"It is not encouraging, but we might make contact through the Stewards, who know both sides, and will see the sense of what we are saying."

"Well, let's get started then," said the bright young man, already impatient. "Where do we find the Stewards?"

"They come to the estates three or four times a year," said another. "That is when we can start talking to them. Show them we have a good market for more good wool and see where that leads to."

There was general nodding and inarticulate noises of assent.

Charles had the last word, as so often, "I earnestly hope the lords will hear their Stewards. I don't know when the restless dissatisfaction in the villages, will break out into violence, or how long it can be contained. Let us talk to the Reeves also, in all our neighbouring villages, who can also put pressure on the stewards. God be with you all for we have urgent work."

CHAPTER TEN

Passion and Riot.

Edith's boys were growing into strong and confident young men ranging the countryside of north Wiltshire quite widely, buying here and selling there. The farming cousins were a few years younger yet there was a very strong bond between them. Despite the age gap the cousins enjoyed each other's visits between market days, when Edith's boys travelled around the villages north of Calne, offering to buy anything they might be able to take to market. When time permitted, they would call into White Clyffe often stopping for an extended meal then driving back to Compton in the dark.

Cedric, the eldest boy was quite a bright young lad and his mother said he wrote a very good hand. He was the leader of his younger brothers, getting into trouble and usually getting out of it again. His father thought his abundant confidence might be the undoing of him. He helped his father in dealing with the cheese factors from an early age learning how to assess cheese quality and which cheeses to offer to a particular buyer. When his father could spare him, he would visit local markets, sometimes helping Edith and Judd, though Edith was careful not to teach him too much in case he set up as a rival. However, he could not help noticing how much money a single cheese could be sold for and compared this with the prices he received from the factors.

Sooner or later he discussed this with his father, who had no interest in retailing. The older man pointed out that the number of cheeses they produced from their growing herd of cows would soon need an army of market sellers travelling right across Wiltshire and perhaps into Bath and Bristol.

"Better we concentrate on our own job and do that well, than try to be a master of two trades." The boy understood his father's reservations but thought him a bit timid, as sons often do.

As the younger brothers, Henry and Bryce came into the farm, the older boy spent more time in Calne, soon making friends with people working in the cloth trade. He gradually learned that wool was more variable than cheese and these variations arose from the feeding conditions as much as from the breed of sheep. The finest wool was grown on the barest pastures such as the high chalk downs or the Cotswolds.

"Father, our ground will not grow the best wool here whatever breed we use."

"Well I've known that all me life, but I'm glad you understand it. Who are you talking to?"

"Oh, there is a wool broker in Calne, and he has told me a lot already."

"Why don't you work there for a few months, now we are not so busy?"

"I have thought about that, but worried that you might be angry."

"No, no; knowledge will never do you any damage."

Cedric soon arranged to live with the wool broker. There were two other apprentices in the house who were senior in the pecking order; one quiet and receptive to other people's suggestions, the other inclined to think he knew it all already. This lad was inclined to be hasty and careless and seemed to attract more criticism from the owner. He sensed that a third apprentice might be one too many and was worried that the new lad might soon have his place.

The wool broker sensed the tension too, and took Cedric with him on the wagon, when he went out to visit a regular supplier of wool. After a lengthy period of conversation, most of it irrelevant to the job in hand, a deal was struck, rough hands were slapped in agreement and money was passed over.

The wagon was loaded, and they returned to Calne, only stopping to eat at the alehouse. The conversation in the bar repeatedly turned to the trade for wool, and many villagers had a few sheep of their own.

"Price of wool goin' up now maister?"

"Aw, no, still plenty about round ere I'd say."

"Hant been no shearin done for a long time. Price usually starts to go up about now."

"Ah but don't leave it too long, or you'll be up against the glut."

"Ah I spose that's right. I got some wool in my shed. If I bring it to ee in Calne, you'd offer a price, I spose?"

"Yea, yea that'll be awright."

Cedric was soaking in the atmosphere of all this and loved the chit-chat and the lively buzz of trade, so was disappointed when he was told to go outside and mind the horse. A soft wind from the south-west blew a scud of drizzle across him so he stood on the dry side of the horse, shivering till he became accustomed. After an age, it seemed, the wool broker emerged, red of face and anxious to get his wool back to Calne. Cedric thought this a bit ironic. These were happy months and stimulating for the apprentices, who slept in an attic at the top of the big house. They were well fed by the household staff overseen by the wool brokers wife; big meals and long working days usually meant they were soon yawning for sleep.

There was plenty of chat during the working day and the older men would tease and bait the three younger lads; beer, sex, and politics were the main subjects. Social change was in the air and slightly simplistic young men were apt to welcome change as an inevitable improvement. But even older people with long heads were frustrated by ancient restrictions and a groundswell of broad opinion responded to a deep dissatisfaction. Wherever people gathered, grumbles about the weather, market conditions, the disgusting habits of new neighbours soon gave way to deeper resentment of aristocratic control.

The broad sense of unhappiness was lifted to new heights of outrage by increased bouts of taxation to fund the failing wars against the French during the declining years of Edward III. Richard, his grandson, came to the throne aged only ten years in 1377. The country was governed by a council of aristocrats who introduced the first and most severe of three poll taxes taking in everyone above the age of fourteen. This wholly new concept struck every family in the country and was a bitter shock.

The third poll tax in five years brought the population to breaking point. The anger was unanimous; meetings were held in Chippenham, Calne, Trowbridge and Warminster. Some people followed the ring leaders from town to town, eventually arriving at Salisbury. Cedric joined in enthusiastically often speaking in support, writing posters in his own hand, too excited to heed the danger. His younger brothers were working on the farm and knew little of his activities, but the wool merchant in Calne was worried that Cedric might be getting in too deep. He knew Edith and asked her to speak to Morris, perhaps to get him back on the farm again till things quietened down. But it was too late. The family had not seen him for many weeks and could find no-one who knew his whereabouts.

Unknown to the apprentices, businessmen were meeting regularly, and they hoped secretly, to find a way forward. The greatest resentment was aimed at the great landowning families who seemed unassailable; if there was a hope, it was the young King might intervene.

The cloth trade in Wiltshire and Somerset was growing into an important industry. Its leaders were the clothiers, a few of whom would become extremely wealthy. Even at this early phase of industrial growth the clothiers were growing in confidence. Increasingly, Salisbury was becoming a marketing centre for west-country woollens, strengthened by easy access to the port of Southampton. Charles, currently based west of Bridgewater, frequently travelled to the city where he had need for permanent accommodation and secure storage.

Forward looking members of the cloth trade throughout both counties had been pressing the stewards to modernise the ancient structure in the agricultural villages with limited success, but the rising rage threatened to set this to nothing. Again, it was the Stewards who possessed the broadest experience of daily life in the villages and a matching understanding of the thinking of the aristocratic landowners; they entertained no hope of change.

Few, if any, at village level understood the King's enormous need for income after a long and crippling period of war. The traditional 'feudal' sources of income from the rural estates now only provided one third of the sum required, taxes on wool exports generated a further third and direct taxation in the form of annual levies on the movable goods of the richest made a further contribution. But still this was not enough; hence the extraordinary attempt to tax the poorest people of working age.

Returning home from Salisbury one evening, Charles clattered into his yard splashed with mud, weary, saddle sore and mightily relieved to reach the comforts of home. He had hardly sat by the fire and shed his boots before he was told, "Your Priest was here earlier today, you know."

"Is he here now?"

"No. He did not remain long. Jenny may know more than I do," said his wife clearly conveying her disapproval.

"Well it is too late to do anything tonight."

Worried by his drooping eyelids, his wife skilfully removed his pot of ale before it crashed to the floor. He slept heavily for an hour and had to be woken to eat his supper.

In the morning after spending time with the men in the yard, he rode out again heading for Bridgewater thinking the Priest cannot get far in a few hours and will probably be preaching to any handy group of people he might find. He had got no further than Cannington when he saw a knot of people standing in the road; he had found his Priest. He walked his horse for a few minutes to let him cool down after a hard ride, then having let him drink and graze beside the road he walked towards the Priest's audience.

The Priest was in good form and had them laughing at his insults to the powerful and mighty. Spotting Charles, he then whipped into his concluding remarks offering hope and an opportunity of better times ahead for the good and faithful. They walked together to the horse and led it to a hitching rail by the Inn. Two hours later, well fed and content, they chatted comfortably.

"I hope you will call in to see me when you can. I shall be in the area for the next week or so," said Charles.

"I plan to be in and around Bridgewater for a few days, so I'll come back your way."

"I have a book you might like to read. I bought it in Salisbury only a few months since, it is called *Piers Plowman*. Do you know it?"

The Priest shook his head, "No but I'd like to see it."

A few days later the Priest arrived in good time for the main meal. Jenny, elated in his company, bustled around busily. After a good but plain meal, two or three conversations competed for attention, to Charles' irritation. He left his seat and went out of the room. In a few minutes he returned to stand with his back to the fire and waited while the conversation lapsed to an apprehensive silence. Charles opened the book at a page he had already marked. He read aloud, as people did, but haltingly, reflecting on the meaning of the written word. After a few minutes he passed it to the Priest, who turned a few pages and read a passage to Charles in a fluent and expressive tone. It was a clear music to all in the room and though few would remember the individual words, they carried their delight away with them.

CHAPTER ELEVEN

A Missing Nephew.

After the rebellion, Cedric's aunt Edith went to Salisbury to make enquiries. She had been to Devizes market but instead of returning to Compton had continued to Amesbury where she left her wagon and horses and walked into Salisbury.

Edith had visited Salisbury market as a buyer from time to time, looking for fine woollens or imported wine that she might sell to well-heeled households in the country towns. But on this Tuesday the crowds were small, there was no laughter and people were alert for danger. Slowly more people came on to the streets and a little business was being done. Edith worked the market stalls with a professional interest, chatting expertly and she hoped, disarmingly. Not till she was certain of the person she was talking to, and clear of eavesdroppers, did she mention her lost nephew and never by name.

Few could offer help, but one person gave her the name of someone who might know. Suddenly they heard shouting and six horses, three abreast, burst through a passive crowd of on-lookers, through them and over them; a boy, kicked in the head by an iron shod hoof, died within the hour. The crowd scattered into narrower streets; injured people, some with broken bones, were helped into doorways of shops and houses.

The main market was deserted now, and she could not find the person who had given her a name. How could she find Morris's boy here? Where should she start? She almost despaired. After a while, the stall holders emerged to protect their stock and people began to walk by in ones or twos. Everyone knew the authorities feared a crowd that might become a riot.

Edith strolled up and down, at long last she spotted her informant talking to a strange hunchbacked little man. Edith felt they were talking about her and when he turned away, she glanced at the stallholder who gave her the slightest nod. Edith followed the hunchback at a distance as a he made his way slowly along Fisherton Street, waiting as he wandered into shops, once taking a pot of ale. She continued past the ale house and found a bench to sit on further along.

Now she felt tired, it had been a long walk into Salisbury, and she was depressed by the hopelessness of her search. She dozed and knew not how long, but when she awoke the hunchback was sitting beside her. His voice was distorted by his malformed chest, but his face was kind, "Come with me, I will make you comfortable." Silently she rose to her feet and did not speak till they were in his house and the door was closed.

"You have lost a nephew?"

She nodded.

"I will make some enquiries. You should sleep here while you can."

It was dark when Edith woke, and she was still alone. She lay still, not fully awake, yet not asleep. The street was quiet, the city slept, and later so did she. Sunlight burst through the cracks in the shutters and she jumped up with a start. Where was he, the little hunchback? Could he be trusted? She was hungry and must get some food.

She freshened herself up as best she could and made her way back into the centre of town feeling slightly self-conscious in her homespun clothes and workmanlike shoes. Tailored clothes were becoming quite common in Salisbury and might even be seen in nearby villages. She passed several alehouses before she found one that appealed, then sat at a long table where a few other people were already eating. An older man turned to her, "Sit down here, we got room for a little un."

Edith smiled "Oh, ah, I've always been little."

Her neighbour pushed his plate back and looked at her carefully, "Did you come through the famine?" Edith nodded. "I bet you've seen a lot in your life, then."

Edith responded, "Yes but nothing worse than what I saw yesterday, in the market, when the horses were driven through a crowd of peaceful people."

The table fell silent.

Someone said, "That boy died, you know."

Edith replied, "I feared as much, he went down like a stone. What be this all about?"

Everyone had a view and tried to talk at once. "There've been riots, though not in Salisbury, yet. But in Winchester, we've heard. Two days ago, a troop of horses left in a hurry for Somerset, been summat going on there I daresay."

"But what is worrying them in Salisbury?" asked Edith.

"Well, people have clamoured for freedom. Country people mostly, though a lot of people in the city are still un-free. Tis time for change."

"But it b'aint a time to talk freely," said another man who got up to leave.

"Ah, e's right, "said Edith's neighbour.

Edith nodded, but remained silent; she did not know who to trust.

Her food came to the table and she started to eat. The table gradually emptied, and she sat alone for some while till a girl came to clear her plate.

"You alright?"

Edith, "Yes, just a bit worried. That's all."

"Are you looking for someone?"

"My brother's boy."

"Well, I hope you find 'im."

Edith spent the morning in town before returning to the house to see if the hunchback had returned, but there was no sign he had been in the house at all. Later, in the evening after a rest, she returned to the alehouse, but the serving girl was no longer there.

She sat there with a drink for a while before ordering some food. She ate alone, listening to the next table.

"Ave you heard they killed an archbishop in Lundun?"

"Who done that?"

"I heard they come from Kent."

"Gaw, what be it cummin to?"

Between mouthfuls a stilted conversation continued.

"No wonder they be chargin about ere wi their orses."

A man chewed vigorously, took a deep breath and said, "Mind you they got to gi us our freedom, even in the country. Things can't stay as they were. Everyone knows that. Be they daft to think that can carry on? People can work where they will whatever the landowner thinks."

Putting down his knife, he took up his pot and drank it dry. Banging his pot down on the table he called, "Yer, bring us another one missus, I be dry wi all this talking." He caught Edith's eye and smiled. "I baint used to it zno. You be in from the country, I spec."

Edith nodded and pausing only to remove a tough piece of beef from her mouth, she answered, "Yea, up country a bit. I come in for the market yesterday, but there weren't much to buy this time."

"So, you come to the market regular, then?"

"Not all that often," she replied, feeling cautious again. "I look for fine woollens to sell on again, if I can find 'em right."

"Where do you sell 'em then? Wilton?"

"No, no, further away, beyond Warminster and Imber. So, I don't get here very often."

"Your pot be empty. Let I get you another." He glanced at the alehouse keeper who had been following the conversation, and Edith wondered how much more he must have heard.

While he was busy with the barrels, she asked quietly, "Is he all right?"

The talkative man slid closer, and whispered, "You never know who to trust round ere." Then louder, "Tis a nice city on a warm summers night, I could show you the sights, if you like."

Edith nodded, "Tis a bit quiet on me own."

They strolled between fine buildings, on a warm still night; Edith paused on the bridge to look down into clear chalk stream water. "So much nicer when it is quiet."

Her new friend replied "I grew up in Stapleford and played in the river there when I were a boy. They were peaceful times."

Edith asked, "How long have you lived in Salisbury?"

"Oh, twenty years, I spec. Just round the corner not far from here. Would you like to see where I live?"

Edith looked closely at him, "I would, but not tonight. I must get back to my friend who lives alone."

She moved closer and leant against him, giving him a friendly squeeze. He bent his head towards her, and she kissed him full on the mouth, rather longer than necessary she thought.

The talkative man was not discouraged and said, "Well I'll look out for you at the market then, and I hope we meet again."

She smiled and turned away, thinking he would surely be in the same alehouse tomorrow.

In another place a short muscular man with a bald head and bulging eyes was still working. A humourless man and implacable, he worked with meticulous care. Everyone in Salisbury knew him and sensed his menace, but more dangerous were the people they did not know, the people he controlled. People like themselves, owners of small businesses, stall holders, travellers, and tinkers. He had a hold on some of these people and knew their weaknesses and vulnerability; they were his spies.

Somewhere deep in the city, the spymaster was taking a firm line with one of the spies who had reported to him, but most of his information was stale. In desperation the timid young man remembered a small woman who has been asking for her nephew in two or three places.

The spy-master demands, "Who is she?"

"No one knows."

"Well find her again and get her name. We need to know the name of her family. An old woman, she must live nearby. Have you been to Wilton? Does anyone know her there? What else have you got?"

The spy added a few details of other strangers talking to locals.

"Is that it? Is that all you've got?"

The spy held out his hand, "You promised to pay me."

He was thrown a shilling, "Find the old woman and her family and I'll give you five shillings." The spymaster had immediately recognised that the missing nephew could be an arrested suspect.

Next morning Edith woke to find the hunchback had returned and was waiting for her to waken. "Come with me, while there are few people about."

A clear fine morning and a low sun sending long shadows along the street; there is no wind and June is a balmy month to be out at first light. They turn off into a narrow alleyway which gradually swings right-handed, then downhill to jump across an open drain. On the other side the path narrows, climbs steeply and twists again. Briefly the sun is in their eyes till they turn left and left again for a few hundred yards winding this way and that. Now Edith is completely lost, and the sun is in the wrong place. After half an hour in this maze of back alleys they come to a workshop with large doors. Within the large door there is a smaller door which the hunchback opens. The light is dim, but he leads her to the stairs without hesitation. They emerge on to a floor that is clean but sparsely furnished then turn into a narrow passage and further stairs to a higher floor. A door is open to a pleasant room with a window, a chair, and a table.

"Someone will bring you some food and water. You will be safe here, and when we can get you back to your horse and wagon, we will do so. Try to be patient."

With that the hunchback was gone.

After two days enjoying the safety and boredom of the clothier's house, Edith was called down to a private room on the first floor. A well-dressed man with a gentle voice asked "How are you Edith? I hope you have recovered from the rough experience on your first day in the city."

She thanked him for his kindness, but was still anxious for her nephew, "Do you have any news of Morris's boy?"

"We know he spoke at meetings at Calne and Wilton and put up posters he had written himself. He was enthusiastic and spoke well with passion. People listened to him but some of those listening may have been spies. Many people have disappeared from Salisbury, but we think some have escaped into the country, so there is still hope."

"And if he has not escaped?"

"Then the military have him. So far they have released no-one."

Edith knew his chances of survival were poor and the clothier read her face. He also knew she too might be captured and questioned, even tortured; he could not risk giving her any more information. He held a small book between the palms of his hands, the fingertips touching lightly, as if in prayer. He laid the book down.

"Edith your horses are ready at the farm where you left them, and we will take you to them in the morning."

The clothier's wagon went up-river to Amesbury at dawn and was clear of Salisbury before the sun rose. Before Amesbury, Edith and her companion were put down in a wooded area and walked into the trees waiting to see if they had been followed. After half an hour they walked to the farm, her companion explaining that her wagon was enclosed and tied down securely because it contains the carcases of animals that have died of a highly infectious form of murrain. "Continue north along the valley and someone will meet you in Ludgershall to take the carcases to a safe burial pit. Do not allow anyone to look inside the wagon. Someone's life depends on it."

When they reached the wagon, the farmyard was deserted; her friend was nowhere in sight.

She walked around the wagon and checked her horse's feet before climbing up to the seat.

"There is enough food and water for your journey. You have been a great help to the movement and will not be forgotten. When we have news of your nephew, we will send it to your family."

Edith took the team and wagon out of the yard and followed the lane leading to the main road. Here she turned north for Amesbury. The stench from the dead animals was strong and she pitied the person inside the covered wagon. In Amesbury, people recoiled from the smell and looked at her with contempt. Most crossed the road to get away, perhaps fearful of what they might catch.

She continued north up the river valley, passing through village after village. Country people quickly closed their doors and shuttered the windows; they knew the smell of death. Once in a quiet place she stopped to give the horses a drink. She thought she heard a groan from inside the wagon and listened carefully. Then she heard a voice say quietly "Help me."

"All right don't make any noise."

She looked around but there was no-one in sight, so she loosened the ropes behind her seat and pulled the sheets apart, then recoiled at the putrid stench. When she dared look, she could see a man's mouth and nose pressed to the opening desperately breathing fresh air. She loosened the ropes and made the opening wider and then she saw his eyes; those amazing hypnotic eyes, first seen in Calne many years before.

"Thank you, God, thank you Mother," he muttered hoarsely.

"Well it's only Edith, but we have met before."

"I can hardly see, my eyes are streaming and painful."

"Do you have anything to drink?" Edith asked.

"No, it has all been spilt now."

"I'll get you some from the river."

She dipped her pot into the horse bucket and passed it to him and he drank heavily. She passed him another and he bathed his eyes. She poured some over his forehead and lightly ran her fingers over his face, repeating this with more and more water.

He pushed through the opening and lifted his arms up to the back of her seat.

"Careful, we don't know if anyone is watching. I'll sit in front of you."

He rested his head against her back and shoulders, breathing heavily through his nostrils. His wet hair dripped down her neck inside her clothes and she arched her back involuntarily. After half an hour she said, "I'll find somewhere safe for the night, then you can come out of that stinking hole."

They rattled on for another hour before she found somewhere safe and secluded. He leapt out of the wagon and walked along the narrow track between stunted hawthorn but was back in a few minutes.

"Let's dump these foul carcases. There's a suitable place just along from here."

Edith drove the team as he directed and backed the wagon into an area of rough ground off the track. The Wandering Priest opened the covers and dragged the decaying bodies from the wagon. They returned to the hidden glade, un-hitched the horses and watered them, then hobbled them to let them graze safely. The bread was getting a bit stale now and the beer was not very good, but the river water nearby was clear enough to drink. Afterwards he bathed in the river and washed his clothes, hoping to remove the odours. While the clothes dried, they lay together under two old horse blankets for warmth.

Edith said, "Tomorrow we will have to head east to get across to the Bourne valley and Ludgershall."

"Who told you about Ludgershall?"

"The clothier, and his man who took me to collect the wagon and horses."

"So that is four people who know. We'll change that plan then only two will know."

He clung to her under the stars and a thin, weak moon, aching for a lost mother. When Edith awoke in the morning he had already left. Edith moved slowly making ready for the journey back to Calne without enthusiasm. She harnessed the horses and hitched them to the wagon. They were a fine old pair of horses and good companions; Bonny nuzzled her shoulder and softly nibbled her heavy cloak. Edith lowered her face to breathe gently into her nostril and enjoyed the warm grassy smell from Bonny's breath. You could trust a horse; they didn't leave you in the night without saying 'God be with you.' Yet, dependable as they were, they could not ease the deep unrequited pelvic hunger.

Edith felt a profound weariness but forced herself to clear everything up and to leave no traces that could connect her to the decaying carcases nearby. She scrubbed out the wagon and folded the covers to let the smells escape. There was an urgent need to get to Morris; her brother would be anxious to know about his son. The horses were driven hard across the Pewsey Vale to Devizes and onward over the high chalk to Calne.

She returned to her brother with nothing to give him comfort; the boy's mother and sisters wept. Morris sat quietly, "It don't sound very good for him, however we look at it."

It was late in the day and Edith accepted the offer of staying the night. She had eaten little since dawn and after a hot thick pottage and maslin bread she was struggling to keep her eyes open.

"Will you have a nice bit of cheese, Edith?" but she hesitated out of politeness.

"Oh, go on then I know it'll be good. Then I must get me head down."

The next morning, after milking the cows, the family gathered again.

"The cows look well, Morris," said Edith brightly, using a time-honoured compliment expected throughout the dairy districts.

"Ah, we've had a good spring for grass," he replied modestly, "but how are your sheep doing?"

"Oh, some of them have been milking since March, they'll be drying off soon."

Peronell asked, "Who has been milking them while you have been away? I think I'd like to try milking sheep."

"Well you have to be young and supple to bend down that low, so I suppose you will get down quite well," said Morris. "Be difficult for your big boys, I reckon Edith."

Edith wondered where the conversation was going, were they trying to take over her flock of sheep, she wondered.

"Oh, we manage awright."

Morris smiled at his cagey old sister, a shrewd and canny market dealer to her bootstraps.

But Peronell persisted, "If you ever need a helping hand, I'd be glad to give it a try."

Edith smiled her thanks but changed the subject.

"One thing I should have mentioned last night, is there was no serious violence in Salisbury, unlike some other places, so people might be released in time."

Peronell's large eyes brimmed with tears at the thought of her brother locked up and her younger sister had to wipe her nose quite bravely.

Edith continued, "There is some talk that the best of the young men, have been taken to Southampton to serve in the navy, so we have to keep hoping and praying for him."

Thank you, Edith for trying to find him for us," said Morris. "But we must keep this to ourselves, so no one links the family to the revolt. These are dangerous times."

CHAPTER TWELVE

The Avenger.

In Salisbury the spymaster rose early while it was still dark and walked along the main streets. He needed to know who might be moving at this early hour, but what little traffic he saw was coming into the city. Not till an hour before sunrise in the first faint light of the new day, did he find even a packhorse carrying anything out of the town. And three people in the wagon? What could that mean? Though the rumours were confusing, and some saw no passengers; still it made him ponder.

The Wandering Priest had slipped away again, and no one had the least idea in which direction he went. Nor did anyone know if the military even knew of his existence. He seemed to have the ability to move in and out of the country towns without anyone even noticing; but they listened to his preaching and loved his vision of freedom, even though the freedom seemed to be indefinitely delayed. But no one would be surprised if he should ever re-appear with a fresh and optimistic message.

Charles the clothier lay low apparently keeping busy with work, though a few key people managed to escape through Southampton on small boats laden with woollen cloth. He had foreseen rage and riot but even he was appalled by the vicious retaliation of the young king. He wondered if the king's anger was sustained by the belief that killing too many was better than killing too few. After all, what matters a few peasants more or a few peasants less, though an aching mother might have explained the difference, if anyone cared to listen.

Even in Salisbury people lived in fear of the military. There had been no rioting here nor murders, yet the military took no chances. Any young man in drink, protesting too loudly was beaten to the ground. A group of three or four making a noise and reluctant to go quietly could expect to be dragged off to the cells, perhaps to watch a beating or an execution. After a few days they might be released with the warning that the cells were terribly crowded, and some executions would be necessary to make space; a message that would be relayed across the city in a few hours.

The spymaster was getting less information; people were no longer talking easily and not at all to strangers. His information passed to the military was earning less money, but they were using other sources, studying traffic to Southampton for example.

The clothiers were exporting increased quantities of Salisbury Ray, a woven cloth, through

Southampton alongside greater quantities of raw wool. Larger ships from the Mediterranean were unable to dock at the London Wool Wharf and were using the deep-water port at Southampton; though still much less busy than the London to Calais trade, the Hampshire port was expanding quickly.

Traffic between Salisbury and Southampton was heavy and wanted men might be loading cloth into boats then remaining on board to assist with unloading on the other side. Charles the clothier was breaking into this trade to supplement the income from his small weaving business in Somerset but had not yet attracted the attention of the authorities.

There had been no more meetings among the clothiers of Somerset and the Stewards of local estates during the weeks of violence, which would have caused alarm. Demonstrations at Bridgewater had turned violent and men had been rounded up indiscriminately and hardly investigated before they were imprisoned or executed. There had been two murders here and the rioters had burned records copying the events in London two weeks earlier, giving rise to fears that a coherent national organisation was in place. Bridgewater was fined as heavily as any town in England, so the violence had probably been aided at the highest level within the town.

Charles did not wish to be linked with activities in Somerset while this continued, so remained in

Salisbury purchasing his supplies of wool through local merchants. He was anxious for the fate of his family and workers and had sent messages by trusted friends, often by an indirect route avoiding Bridgewater entirely. He urged his wife to go to her family in Dorset and take as many of her household as she might.

He knew his weaving loom would be idle and unattended. With neither work nor wages, his men would have no alternative but to return to their home villages, perhaps to work on the farms in return for food and a roof over their head. Charles hoped desperately that none of them would have been swept up in the passion and rage of the moment but feared for their safety.

Throughout the summer and autumn, the military hunted down suspects and active campaigners from Kent to Somerset and north to Beverley and York; a measured estimate suggests possibly one thousand five hundred people died in royal revenge. Not till September, did Charles think it safe to leave Salisbury for Blandford and Iwerne Minster where his wife had spent her childhood and where he hoped she was safe with her family.

Despite misgivings, Charles feels he must go to his wife but though he has sent messages to her, there have been no replies. He does not know if she is well or ill and the tension is slowly eating his mind. He does not know if she is with her brothers at her old home but must go there, though an underlying anxiety blights any anticipated pleasure he might feel.

The journey was uneventful, and late on the second day he arrived at Iwerne and made his journey along the street. Only one person was seen standing by the road, so Charles asked him for the house of William son of Isaac. For a few seconds the young man seemed not to respond, then shook his head slowly to left and right, then left again and lowered his eyes to the ground. There had been no expression in his eyes nor were any words spoken. Charles turned to look at the nearest houses, but no one was visible. He walked his horse to end of the street and back again but not one person appeared. He decided to try the door of the largest house but there was no response to his knocking even when he shouted. He tried four houses before an elderly woman came around the side of her house wanting to know who he was.

"I am Charles and I'm looking for my brother-in-law, William son of Isaac."

"I don't know ee."

"I know he lives in this village, and my wife has been staying with him."

"Thee better ask sumother."

"Where is everyone?"

"Oh, they be about."

"Where?"

"Workin... In the fields. Should be back direckly."

Charles turned his horse around and took it to the end of the village where the road descended to a stream. Here he unhitched the horse and let him drink. When full, the horse reached for a rich and varied clump of reeds. Within minutes a voice shouted, "Ere, they weeds be our'n, not your'n."

Charles looked at the man who was about the right age and asked, "Are you William?"

"I might be, an' who might you be?"

"Well I am Charles and I hope my wife has been safe with you these last terrible weeks."

"Oh ah, we've kep her for ee."

"Is she well?"

"Seemingly. Thee best hitch up the hoss again an goo down the road to the yard."

Charles took the advice and made his way to the farmyard behind his brother-in-law's house. If there was anyone watching his arrival, they did not intend to help him. Some cattle were calling to each other and he walked behind a thatched shed to investigate. Two women in rough country clothes were bringing the animals in from a wooded area beyond a cornfield. Three or four men and boys were cutting what he thought might be oats, tying them into sheaves then standing them up in small groups to dry in the wind.

The women turned to each other when they saw him, but he could not even guess what they were saying. As they drew closer, he recognised Ethel, his wife. Her hair appeared not to have been washed or combed and she was wearing rough homespun garments he had never seen before. Charles knew better than to disturb the cattle before they were safely penned, so did not call out to Ethel, nor did she call to him.

Her face was drawn and gaunt and reddened by the sun. He guessed she had been labouring in the fields with her family and other people from the village. He went towards her and made to put his arms around her, but she shrank from him.

"Where have you been all these months?"

"I've mostly been in Salisbury. Did you get my messages?"

"I got one telling me to come here. But have heard nothing more. And have only had the money I brought with me, so I've had to work to pay for my keep."

"Oh, you poor thing; I thought your family would have been kinder."

"They've fed me and housed me, but they don't have very much."

"I'll give them something before we go."

"Go? Where to? Is it safe at the mill?"

"We won't risk going to the mill yet. I heard the military are still hunting the area."

"Well I don't want to go to Salisbury. I don't know anyone there. And I am not going looking like this."

"It might be good cover while we are travelling. No one will know who you are or where you have come from."

During the night Charles was disturbed by Ethel, her body racked by deep silent sobs, though still fast asleep. He felt he was beginning to understand something of her agonies these last few months.

In the morning she briskly sorted the things she had brought from the mill in June and loaded the dog cart. Charles caught the horse, contented after a good nights grazing, only to find Ethel had disappeared. He got the horse ready and hitched him up to the cart and waited for Ethel. At length she reappeared from the direction of the church, her face ravaged and unable to speak; they rode away from Iwerne Minster in silence.

Before sunset on the second day they arrived in Salisbury, but the city was still busy with most of the weaving shops still banging and crashing as they had since early morning. People were rushing backwards and forwards, not even pausing to talk to an acquaintance. Not even talking usually, but shouting rather, which Ethel though very rude. Charles turned into a side road, then turned again into an open yard between two larger buildings. Ethel was relieved to escape the din of busy streets.

It was a comfort to find a clean bed chamber and soon she shed her filthy country clothes. Some jugs of hot water were brought, and a hip bath was partly filled, a luxury she had not enjoyed for three months. Having washed and combed her hair and dressed in clothes she had carried from their home in Somerset, she was restored. Though extremely tired from two days in an open cart on rough and unpredictable roads, she felt strong enough to face new challenges. They ate lightly together and retired to bed within the hour.

Before the sun rose, Ethel was disturbed by an unfamiliar sound, the din and racket of a city at work. Charles was still sleeping heavily, and she lay quietly, reflecting that if she was tired, he must be doubly so. When he stirred, she touched his hand lightly and turned to him, "You have slept well. Do you feel better?"

"Much better for the sight of your smiling eyes."

Later they discussed the business.

"Charles how much have we lost, these last few months?"

"I don't know how bad things are in Somerset, but there was unsold cloth, I know. And that may be ruined or stolen, perhaps."

Ethel nodded, "Yes they were foot-fulling in the stream all the week before I got away. Another cloth on the loom, half finished, I expect; and several weeks weaving since we sold anything."

Charles was silent but Ethel persisted, "How have things gone here in Salisbury?"

"Well we have a small loom here, and wool is more expensive from the brokers, though it takes much less of my time. So, I can concentrate on producing cloth for the local market which is a different trade. I am selling enough cloth to pay all the bills so we can keep this going till it is safe to return to Somerset."

"You can't be producing very much on one small loom."

"No, but there are a lot of independent weavers here in Salisbury; I could double my sales and more, quite easily. I already have five or six spinners working from their own homes. I think we should manage a steady expansion till we can start up again at the old place."

Charles looked steadily at Ethel and reflected this was more like the old girl he knew. What a difference a bath and a change of clothes makes.

At White Clyffe, in deep countryside, such luxuries were not expected, and a certain doggedness was a basic requirement. Edith, familiar with life in town and country, took care with her appearance but was still an independent working countrywoman who dressed for work and strenuous work at that. But that tough exterior concealed a lonely heart, and no-one had been close to her in the years since Judd had died.

In her solitary moments she sometimes found herself wondering what the talkative, friendly man might be doing in Salisbury. In any case she had not been to Salisbury Market since June, so there was a need to build up a stock of fine woollens, after all. Winter was coming and it was sensible to make use of the last bit of fine weather, while she could. Really it was a perfectly justifiable business decision and of course her sons would see the sense of it.

Tomorrow she would ride to see Morris. Perhaps Peronnell would like to come back with her to mind the sheep while she was away. Her last conscious thoughts before she slipped into sleep, she was beside the talkative man, leaning over the bridge and looking down to the clear stream, near the house he had invited her to visit.

READER'S RESPONSE

Please respond to: colin@foxhangers.co.uk

Dear Reader,

Thank you for choosing to read White Clyffe. Book publishing is a new experience for me, but I am learning fast. I am already sure the most valuable information will be your views and experience.

After spending six months writing a book it is quite difficult to place myself in the position of someone who has picked up the book and read it for the first time. Your first impressions will be extremely interesting to me.

All suggestions for improvement will be most helpful. Naturally, I hope your experience was enjoyable, but if not, I need to know that too.

I have more books planned so this is a great opportunity to learn from the ultimate judge. Thank you for your response.

Best Regards,
Colin Fletcher.